I0564684

Verner Zevola Reed

Tales of the Sun-Land

Verner Zevola Reed

Tales of the Sun-Land

ISBN/EAN: 9783744753562

Printed in Europe, USA, Canada, Australia, Japan

Cover: Foto ©Andreas Hilbeck / pixelio.de

More available books at **www.hansebooks.com**

TALES OF THE SUN=LAND

By VERNER Z. REED
Author of "LO-TO-KAH"

Illustrated by
L. MAYNARD DIXON

"In the sad Southwest, in the mystical Sun-land,
Far from the toil, and the turmoil of gain;
Hid in the heart of the only—the one land
Beloved of the Sun, and bereft of the rain."

MDCCCXCVII
CONTINENTAL PUBLISHING CO.
New York and London

To My Wife
MARY DEAN REED

CONTENTS

ILLUSTRATIONS

AN ENCHANTED NIGHT

 PARTY of overland travelers were one night seated in the little bar-room of a country hotel in the western border of Arizona. To pass the time, they indulged in story-telling. The stories finally drifted into tales of goblins, ghosts and spooks, and one gentle-man related the following tale, which he declared was a true one, and which he called:

"AN ENCHANTED NIGHT."

Through the slow hours of a hot August day I had ridden along heated, dusty roads, and at night I stopped at a lonely house in a little valley to seek shelter and food for myself and my tired horse. As I reined up in front of the house I saw no sign of life; not a man or a woman or a horse or a cow or a fowl or any living thing could be seen, and the melancholy quiet that was settling over the place was oppressive. However, there was no other house for a long distance. A storm was brewing, the night was upon me. I and my horse were weary and hungry, and I halloed lustily to learn if this strange place were inhabited. After I had called loudly several times, an old, old woman came to the door. She was bent almost double and her flesh was of the yellow-parchment color so often seen in people of extreme age. Her thin, white hair floated about her head and her jaws were continually working as though she were unceasingly mumbling to herself. She looked at me with a vacant expression, and was turning to hobble into the house again when I asked if I could have lodging for the night.

She muttered some words that I took for an assent, and beckoned me into the house. An old man, wearing a tasseled cap upon his head and leaning upon a cane, tottered out upon the porch. He shaded his eyes with his hand and looked at me for a moment, then he turned away and called out:

"Jade, jade, come here!"

In answer to his call a being in the form of

The tall house in the valley.

a woman came to the house from a little grove
near by. She was tall and ungainly, with brutal
features and muscular limbs, apparently about
forty years of age, barefooted, bareheaded, and
clad only in a short, ragged skirt of some rough
material, and a torn waist. Her grayish-red
hair fell unkempt over her bare shoulders; her
eyes rolled as though she were in a fit; her bony
hands clasped and unclasped themselves spas-
modically, and a thin, white, frothy foam was
gathered at her mouth. She stared at me for a
moment and then tossed her shaggy head and
uttered the wildest, uncanniest, ghostliest laugh
I had ever heard; all the time clasping and un-
clasping her hands, and quivering and jerking
all over her body like one with the dance of St.
Vitus.

"Idiot," said the old man to her, "stable
and feed the stranger's horse!"

She snatched the reins from my hand and
ran off toward the stable, running so fast that
the horse galloped to keep pace with her. The
old man then turned to me and said:

"The idiot will tend your horse well; have
no fear. Come in."

I followed him into the house, which was a

tall, wooden building with large windows. The inside was but poorly furnished, there being no carpets on the floors, no pictures or papering on the walls, and only such articles of plain furniture as were absolutely necessary.

The old man gave me a chair, and then he and the old crone sat mumbling and muttering to themselves, and paying no heed to me whatever. Soon the crazy woman returned from stabling my horse, and filled the room with her wild laughter. The old man ordered her to prepare supper, and she writhed and shambled out of the room, but soon put her head in at the door again, and the old man, saying the single word "Supper," went into the next room; I followed him, and was followed in turn by the mumbling old woman.

The meal was served on a plain deal table, and consisted of wild berries, fruits, uncooked vegetables and water. The lunatic sat opposite me and continually caused my blood to run cold with her peals of weird laughter, that rose sometimes to a shriek, and then quavered and trembled like the hopeless moan of a lost soul.

Supper was soon finished, and I partially quieted my unstrung nerves with a pipe, and then told the old man that I should like to retire. He called to the crazy woman, pointed to me, and said, " Bed." The lunatic took up a candle and led the way through a door and up a winding, creaking stair-case. As soon as we had reached the first landing she executed a veritable demon's dance about me, clutching at me with her talon-like hands, and screeching and howling like a very devil. I feared she would attack me, but she turned and led the way up another stairway and into a large, bare room, and then, after making one more savage lunge at me, she turned and ran screeching down the stairs.

The uncanniness of the place and people had completely unstrung my nerves, and I sank trembling and exhausted into a chair. I was in a very large room that contained only the chair and a bed that looked like a bier. The storm had not come up, and the moon, which had now risen, cast queer shadows upon the bare, white walls, and a long, white curtain floated in the breeze that blew through the open windows. As soon as I had in a measure regained my composure, I bolted fast the door and felt more secure than I had since entering that strange house. If I could have stolen out unobserved and taken my horse, I would have gone away and ridden all night rather than stay in that horrible place, but the fear of encountering the lunatic, and an uncertainty about being able to find my horse, detained me, so I undressed and threw myself wearily upon the bed. My tired muscles and unstrung nerves soon succumbed to nature's call, and I fell asleep and must have slept an hour or more.

I awoke suddenly with a strange feeling that some one was in the room. I arose in the bed, on my elbow, and looked around me. The moon had gone almost down, leaving the room nearly dark, and the shadow of the flapping curtain moved darkly up and down the wall. The breeze had grown cooler and stronger and was blowing refreshingly into the room. The oppressive heat was gone, and to make myself more comfortable I pulled another sheet over me and then lay back upon the pillow, but not asleep. After lying quietly for a little while, I heard a low, faint sigh at the side of my bed. What new horror was I to encounter in this place of bewitchment? I gathered my courage,

opened my eyes, looked at the place from
whence the sigh seemed to come, but saw
nothing. Thinking my over-wrought nerves
had excited my imagination and led me into
error, I again lay down upon my pillow and
once more closed my eyes. Then again I heard
the sigh, this time beginning near my face and
seeming to rise toward the ceiling, and grow
fainter as it rose. I shuddered, and kept my
eyes closed in fear. My senses had not deceived
me this time, for the sound was unmistakable.
Cold drops of perspiration broke out upon me,
my blood seemed to chill in my veins, and my
flesh to creep on my bones. Once again I heard
the sigh, but nearer and more distinctly than
before, and I seemed to feel a light, cold breath
upon my throat. I covered my face with the
sheet, but again I heard the sigh, stronger than
before, and it ended in an almost unintelligible
whisper of the word : "Claderven." In very
desperation I uncovered my head and opened
my eyes, and there by my bed I saw a white,
filmy, misty object, whose shape I could scarcely
make out in the darkness.

It hovered for a moment between the bed
and the ceiling, and then seemed to condense

and come closer to me, and I could distinctly hear the whispered word "Claderven." My terror was leaving me, and I sat upright in the bed and looked at the being. As I looked, it assumed more definite shape, and I could dimly discern the outline of a face and two cold, staring eyes. I put out my hand to it, and said:

"Demon, spirit, wraith, whatever you are, what do you want with me?"

Again came the whispered word "Claderven," floating like a breath of air in the room; a hand was stretched to me from the misty form, and a hollow voice said: "Take my hand."

I took the outstretched hand in mine; it was cold and clammy within my clasp, and caused cold chills to run up and down my body. But as I held the hand, the form of the wraith grew more and more distinct; the features took on the rounded outline of a woman's face; the hand and arm grew warm, and the eyes began to sparkle.

"Being," said I, "what are you?"

"Claderven, I am thy lover, Zorah," she slowly replied, in a low voice.

" Once more the hand grew warm within my clasp. "

"But my name is not Claderven, and I have never known anyone named Zorah," I replied, releasing the wraith's hand which I had held.

Instantly the form grew dim again, the color left the face, the lustre faded from the eyes, and when she spoke again her voice was very weak.

"Hold my hand again," she said, "for all my strength comes from you. Hold my hand and I will talk with you."

Again I took the clammy hand, which once more grew warm within my clasp, and the face and eyes beamed with life again. I could see her white, beautiful bosom gleaming and heaving beneath her robe of mist, and she said to me:

"You are Claderven to me, whatever your name may now be upon the earth. Twelve long centuries ago, in a sunny land in the East, you and I were lovers. You died, and on account of some sin you had committed, you were condemned to be born again upon the earth, and forget your first life; but when I died—which was from grief for you—I lived among the spirits, grieving for you ever, and thereby incurring the mighty displeasure of those who rule

that life, for allowing my longings to go down-
ward to an earthly love.   Long years I have
been separated from you, wearing my soul away
in almost hopeless hope of ever finding you.
For you I have been sorely punished, and made
to be of the vile of the earth.   But to-day I find
you, and to-night I come to you as a bride
comes to the couch of her lord after a long
waiting.   Kiss me and fill me with the strength
of your life, and see how fair your Zorah is."

She pressed her lips to mine, and seemed to
drink in my very breath, and as she kissed me
her form expanded into perfect womanhood.
Her fair proportions, delicately moulded, were
yet strong as steel; her breast rose and fell in
ecstasy, and her eyes sparkled with the light of
love.   The very elements seemed to grow beautiful with her; perfume floated in the air, and
soft sounds, like the strains of distant music,
fell upon the hearing.   She twined her rounded
arms about me, and from then I took no heed
of time, and knew not how long we had been
thus till a voice was heard near us.   On
looking, we saw a shadowy form that rose
majestically beside us. Zorah covering her face
in her hands, wept, and begged the forgiveness

of the being, which seemed to be a ruler. With
a look of great sorrow, it said:

"Zorah, fair of form but lewd of heart, go
again and mingle with the low and mean of the
earth; to be the lowest of the low, the despised
of all. To-day the time of your punishment was
ended; to-night again you broke the command; go again!"

Immediately after he had spoken I heard the
shrieking laugh of the idiot below stairs, and
Zorah and the spirit had faded from my view.
The many strange incidents of the night had
completely overcome me and I fell asleep and
slept until I was awakened by a loud pounding
on the door. I arose to find that the morning
had dawned, and the sunlight was streaming
through the window. I hastily dressed and
descended the stairs. In the lower hall I met
the idiot, who was shrieking and moaning there.
When I came to her she ceased her screaming;
for a little while her face stopped writhing, and
in a low voice she said to me:

"I am Zorah. This form and this derange-
ment is my curse, placed upon me in punishment
of my love for you. I had served out the long
years of my expiation, and last night I would

have been free, had not some strange destiny
sent you to me. Now, for a time, the length
of which I do not know, I must again inhabit
this hideous form. Yet I am glad you came; I
had waited long,—I had waited long. You will
come again, sometime, some place, for ours are
kindred destinies! Good bye.''

As she ceased speaking, the light of reason
faded from her face. Her eyes began to roll
again, her mouth to froth; she clutched at me
and might have done me harm, had she not
fallen in a fit upon the floor. I hurried away,
and upon the porch I found the old man; I
offered him payment for my lodging, but he
struck at me with his cane and pointed me to
my horse, which was bridled and saddled ready
for the day's journey.

I rode rapidly away, the horse seeming to be
as eager as I to leave the place, and I did not
stop until I came to a farm house full five miles
distant. The farmer was hoeing in his yard,
and I drew rein and asked him who lived in the
tall house in the valley. He looked curiously at
me, and then called out:

"Ho, wife! Here is another who talks of
the tall house in the valley; or may be it is the

same one with his appearance changed, for I do believe it is all bewitchment."

He was afraid at first, but after some parley he told me that once every year, during the hot days of August, a stranger rode by his farm with troubled looks on his face, and made strange inquiries about a tall house in the valley.

"And there is no tall house in the valley," said the farmer, "for in this scantily settled region I know every house for full twenty miles, and there is none such as you describe, unless the devil rears it in the night, to work his evil there, and causes it to vanish in the day."

THE CARIB QUEEN

THE CARIB QUEEN.

 NE sultry day I was wandering aimlessly about the dusty back streets of Ciudad Juarez. A few half-naked children were lying on the ground, asleep in the sun. Occasionally a policeman in a dirty white uniform slouched by me with his big revolver swinging at his side. A burro train loaded with fagots was ambling down the street in charge of a woman and a boy; and a motionless Mexican, with his sombrero pulled over his eyes, was leaning listlessly against an adobe wall.

I spoke to the man, and he bowed, but he did not remove his hat as the *peons* always do. After he had bowed he turned his eyes from me to vacancy, and seemed to forget my existence. I was tired, however; there is but little shade in Juarez, and I determined to share the shelter of that wall with the man and make him talk.

When I had given him a Vera Cruz cigar and a
drink from my flask he deigned to take an interest in me, and after I had sat under the wall
with him for an hour he told me a story. The
story may not be true, and it certainly seems
improbable; but the telling of it had a strange
effect upon the man, and he told it in seeming
sincerity; so I think after all it may not be
wholly false. The story is written here in the
man's own words, just as he told it to me that
day while the slanting rays of the burning sun
were shimmering mercilessly down upon the
mud walls of Ciudad Juarez.

"My name is Pablo Garcia, and I am a man
for whom nature intended better things than
lying idle in the shade of mud walls in a poor
border town. The ancestors of my family can
be traced back in unbroken lines for eight
hundred years, and some of them were the men
who helped to found the kingdom of Castile. I
was born in the City of Mexico and educated in
Spain, and when my father died he held my
hand in his and told me I might, if I willed, be
one day the President of the Republic of Mexico.
It is well that my father died; and it is well
that we poor creatures of the earth have death

to hope for. If we had not that hope we should surely all go mad.

"I was ever an adventurous man. Just after I came from college I joined a revolution against the government, and was made a colonel. It was promised me that I should be the governor of a state. Then my old father came to me with tears in his eyes and besought me not to rebel against a government that was so ready to honor him and his, and for love of him I threw aside my uniform, withdrew from the rebellion, and retired to an hacienda that my father owned in Yucatan. I was to remain there but a few months, until the revolution was over and my father had secured me a pardon, when I was to go to the capital and begin the serious work of manhood.

"Yucatan is a dreary land, unfit for men to live in, and my stay there would have been short indeed, if it had not been for a strange tale I heard there that incited the desire of exploration within my breast. It was rumored in Yucatan that there was a strange city of Indians situated in a remote part of the peninsula, a city where white men had never been and where they were not allowed to go. I could

learn but little of this city; the Indians would
not talk of it, and the white men believed its
existence to be a myth, as white men have but
little faith in the marvelous. I believed the city
existed, and I determined to find it, to enter it,
to learn of its people and their manners and
·customs, and to return to it with soldiers
and make it as free of entrance as any city in
Mexico.

"No one would join me in the expedition, even
the *peons* refusing to go for pay, and I set out
alone. I rode a mule, for only mules can live and
thrive in the *tierra caliente*. I rode for many days
through the desert, sleeping alone on the sands,
or occasionally passing the night in the hut of
some Indian. In time I came to a morass that
seemed to be impassable, and I could not force
my stubborn beast to enter it. I believed that
the unknown city lay beyond this morass, and I
was determined to cross it; so I turned loose
the mule and began to wade in the muddy water.
The morass grew worse as I advanced, and I
often thought I should sink, but I was fortunate
and always managed to save myself by grasp-
ing the branches of trees. Near night I came
to a small tract of land that lay higher than

the water, and I slept there. The next day I struggled onward through the swamp, and at night climbed into a forked tree to sleep, as there was no land that lay above the water.

"In this manner I struggled in that dismal forest swamp for nine days. On the tenth, just as I was ready to give up and die, I came to dry land. I was covered with slime, my feet and limbs were bleeding, my clothes were torn to shreds, I was almost crazed with hunger, and I think I could not have lived out one more day in that desolate jungle. When I reached the dry land I gathered some wild berries and ate them, and then I lay down and slept the sleep of utter exhaustion. I slept for many hours, how many I do not know, and when I awoke I was sore and stiff; but my strength soon partially returned, and I paid but little heed to my plight, for I believed I was near the mysterious city. I cleaned my revolver, washed myself, put my clothing in as good condition as I could, and set out directly into the heart of the forest that lay before me. The forest was so dense that I could scarcely see the sky above me, and I was glad of this, for without the shade the heat would have been unendurable to a weak man on foot.

"I journeyed on for two days more, and then I came to another small swamp. When I had crossed it I began to see signs of human inhabitancy. Footprints were to be seen in the soft earth, I found a shred of a cotton garment, and I soon came to a small field of cotton and Indian maize. I ate some of the maize and slept near the field, and in the morning I was awakened by hearing a great noise like that made by a multitude singing. I then made my way forward with great caution, for I did not know what manner of people I was approaching, and I had heard fearful tales of the ferocity of the Indians who dwelt in the undiscovered city. I made my way stealthily from one tree to another, as a wild Indian makes his way when near an enemy, and at last I came within sight of the city I had risked so much to find.

"The city stood in the center of an open space in the forest, and was surrounded by a wall of heavy masonry. It was about half a mile from the forest line to the city wall, and I feared greatly to enter the open space that lay between, as it was filled with Indians in strange garb, who were dancing. By striking upon the trunks of trees I at last found one that was hollow; and upon climbing the tree I found that I could get inside of it, which I did. Then with my knife I worked to make a hole in the hard wood, but by the time I had cut through the trunk I found that the dance was over and that the Indians had gone within the city wall.

"I remained inside the tree all night, sleeping very comfortably, and was awakened at sunrise by the sounds of the Indians dancing and singing again. There were not many of the Indians when it is remembered that they were all of the inhabitants who dwelt in the city. They numbered about two thousand, men, women and children, and they were different from any Indians I had ever seen. In their dancing they seemed exhausted and ready to drop with weariness, and I afterwards learned that they had danced for four days and had fasted during all that time. I could see that the dance was of a religious nature, as all Indian dances are, and a tall old man with flowing hair seemed to be the chief priest.

"After the dance had continued for several hours the priest and ten men entered the walls of the city. When they returned they bore a huge stone that was shaped like a table, and upon this stone they bound a young Indian boy, who seemed to be of a different tribe. They went again into the city, and when they returned I was greatly surprised to see them leading a white man whose eyes were bandaged. I supposed they were going to kill the white man, and I carefully examined all the chambers of my revolver to see that they were loaded; for, while the Indians were a host against two, I did not intend to see a man of my own blood slain by wanton savages unless I essayed to rescue him. I was just ready to climb out of the tree when the old priest lifted up his hands, and I was greatly astonished to hear him say in as good Spanish as is taught in the college at Madrid:

"'Now, oh, Father Sun, is the soul of an alien to be sent across the great waters to thy land in payment for the continuance of the life of thy daughter, our Queen. From the numbers of our enemies we have taken this boy, whose heart shall bleed for thee; and from the numbers of the white despoilers we have taken a white skinned man who shall be held and sacrificed at the dance of the harvest. The eyes of this boy who lies bound upon the stone shall soon gaze into the eyes of Him-Who-Rules-The-World, and

we send him as a token that we are yet thy
children and are yet faithful. Oh, mighty Father
Sun, grant us the blessing of continued life for
our Queen.'

"None of the Indians seemed to understand
what the priest said, nor *did* they, as I afterwards learned; for Spanish was not taught
to more than three people of that city at one
time.

"When the priest had spoken I believed the
white man was in no immediate danger, and I
remained within the tree. When the sun was
exactly in the zenith the Indians knelt, and the
old priest, with a stone knife, cut out the living
heart of the boy who was bound to the stone,
and cast it, all bleeding, toward the sun. My
blood ran cold at the sight, and I was sorely
tempted to take a shot at the murderous
heathen, but my better judgment told me to
remain quiet.

"After the sacrifice a great feast of maize
and meat was spread, and the people ate like
famished wolves. After they had eaten they went
into the city, some almost falling to the ground
with sleepiness. The priest led the white man
away, the open space was deserted, and when

the sun went down there was not a sound to be heard. I believed the people were all asleep, and I climbed out of the tree and satisfied my hunger upon some of the fragments of food that were left scattered over the ground. I rested for an hour, and then set out to enter the city, determined to solve its mysteries if I lost my life in doing it.

"Just as I reached the gate of the city I met the white captive I had seen in the day. He was stealing along noiselessly, and just as he came outside of the gate I spoke to him. He seemed amazed to be addressed in Spanish. At first he feared it was the old priest, who could speak that language, and he started to run. I called him back, telling him I was a friend, and when he came we went to the edge of the forest to talk. The man told me he was an exile from Cuba, having escaped from a prison in that island, and made his way to the coast of Yucatan in a ship in which he had hidden himself. When he reached Yucatan he left the ship, and after wandering for a long time in the forest along the coast, he was captured by a band of Indians who seemed careful not to hurt him, and who conducted him to the walled city and delivered him to the old priest. In the city he was kept a close prisoner, seeing no one but the priest, and was never taken out of his cell until the day he had been led forth to stand by the boy who was sacrificed. From the old priest he had learned that the people who dwelt in the city were Caribs who had fled from their island home in the West Indies four hundred years ago. These Caribs were ruled by a white queen, and it was believed that the life of the queen was prolonged if human sacrifices were made to the sun. The queen was not allowed to marry nor to look upon any living person but the priest, and her successor was provided by capturing white girls from the Mexican cities. The white race had driven the Caribs from their ancestral island home, and they believed that the whites had a right to rule them; but they believed that if they submitted to a white ruler they would do right to kill all other white people who invaded their land.

"The Cuban told me all this, and said he had stolen away when the old priest who guarded him had fallen asleep. He begged me to go with him into the swamps and strive to escape, but I would not go until I had entered the city. I thought it safe to enter, as the Cuban said the people were all asleep from fatigue and gluttony, and I prevailed upon him to go with me inside the walls.

"The Cuban had no weapon but a knife, but I had my revolver, and with our weapons in our hands we entered the gate of the sleeping city. The moon was shining brightly and we could see clearly. The houses of the city were joined closely together; they were made of heavy blocks of stone, and it seemed that the city must at some time have held a large population. There were no windows in the houses, light being admitted through holes cut in the walls. The streets were crooked and narrow and were paved with rocks worn smooth by the usage of centuries. There were no animals of any kind to be seen. Great heaps of maize and raw cotton were piled in the streets, and meat, no doubt the flesh of wild animals, was seen hanging on high poles. In one corner of the city was a large building of white stone, of beautiful architecture, upon the walls of which were fine carvings. The Cuban said this was the palace of the queen, which no one but the priest was allowed to enter, as it was sacrilege for the

" We entered the gate of the sleeping city."

Caribs to look upon their ruler. When we had seen this much we feared to stay longer in the city and were retracing our steps toward the gate when we met the old priest. He had awakened from his sleep, had found his prisoner gone, and had started forth in search of him. When he came upon us the Cuban struck him fiercely in the face, and the priest, mad with pain and anger, drove his stone knife into the Cuban's breast. The Cuban fell, but as he fell he caught the neck of the priest in the grip of death and buried his knife in his heart. The two men lay dead in each other's arms, and I stood alone, surrounded by the unknown terrors of that mysterious place.

"While I was wondering how I might best make my escape I heard the noise of men walking near the city gate, and I knew I would be unable to leave the city. I believed I might find safety near the palace of the queen, as the Indians were not allowed to go there, and I took up the body of the dead Cuban and stole toward the palace walls. There was a massive door entering the palace and I tried it to find if it were unlocked. It opened easily and through it I entered a large chamber. I did not know if

I should ever go out of the door alive, but it seemed to me that I had a better chance of life in the palace than I should have in the streets when the people learned that their priest had been killed. The room I was in was very high, the ceiling was pictured, the walls were of the color of pearls, and a soft light came in from small holes in the floor. There was a peculiar fragrance in the room that revived my strength and spirits as though I had drunk of rich old wine. I left that room and entered another that was like a large closet. There I left the dead body of the Cuban, after securing his knife, and returned again to the large chamber. When I had entered, a door was partly opened, and a soft voice said :

" ' Who comes ? '

" The words were spoken in Spanish, and it seemed strange to me to hear my mother tongue in that strange place.

" The voice was the voice of the queen. She thought it was the priest who came, and she bade me enter; and I went through the curtained doorway into a room that seemed like the abode of a fairy. Precious stones were set in the walls and the floor, silken draperies and

couches were all around, and there were figures
and friezes of exquisitely carved white stone.
But I forgot the beauty of the room when I
saw its occupant. I forgot danger; I forgot
the dead Cuban and the dead priest; I forgot
myself; I forgot the world. Ah, Señor, in all
this world there is no woman so beautiful as
was that golden queen of the Caribs! Her skin
was white as the bloom of the lily, her eyes
were like two stars, her long hair was like
molten gold and was soft as fine-spun silk. She
was tall, her form and her limbs were as perfect
as statuary, and her face was the face of an
angel. She reclined upon a silken couch, she
was clad in a clinging silken robe, and in all the
years of my life I never expect to look upon
another woman so fair as she. She looked upon
me in wonder, but not in fear, and she smiled.
Her smile riveted the fetters of love about my
heart, and I was her slave from that time forever. She asked me who and what I was and
whence I came. I know not what reply I made
her then, but I know that, except the old priest,
I was the only man she had ever seen, and she
did not fear me. But when my senses returned
to me I told her who and what I was. I told

her of my journeying in search of her city. I
told her of the Cuban captive and of his death,
and of the death of the priest, and I told her of
Mexico, and of the white people, and of the
world that she had never seen and had never even
heard of. I told her, too, that I was like a wild
animal driven to bay, that the men of her city
would kill me if I went into the streets or tried
to escape, and I knelt and took her hand and
asked her to save my life. She listened to me in
wonder, and marveled much at what I said.
Then she took my hand in hers and promised
she would save my life. She feared, though,
that in the morning, when the people discovered
that the priest was dead, they would make a
great search for his slayer, and might even enter
her palace. I told her of the dead body in the
outer room, and bade her tell the people, if they
came, that the dead Cuban had slain the priest
and had then fled to the palace and died. I
believed then I was safe, for the old priest was
the only Carib who had seen me or known that
I was in the city.

"The queen then asked me many questions,
and her speech to me was in the purest Castilian, that language having been taught to her

"She looked upon me in wonder."

by the priest, as it was the language in which all their worship was performed. The Caribs had learned this language while yet they lived upon their island, and it had been carefully handed down among their priests ever since.

"I talked with the queen all night, forgetting that men ever slept; but in the morning we were disturbed by a summons at the outer door. The queen went into the ante-chamber, where was a man who told her that the priest was dead and that he himself was now priest. He told her a white captive had killed the priest, and that the man could not be found, although all the city had been searched, and he asked if the man had entered the palace.

"The queen told him that the man had come to her palace, that she knew it was not meet that any but the priest should come there, and she had killed the man with her own hands. Then she showed him the dead body of the Cuban in the closet, and the priest believed her and took the body away, saying the Caribs were thrice blessed in having a queen such as she.

"The queen then returned to me, and I was no longer in danger. In all the time I remained in her palace no one ever came but the priest, and he came only to the ante-chamber. I was a thing of great wonder to the queen, as she had never seen a white man before; and we would talk for hours together, our hands clasped, as children talk of fairy tales. Before we knew it, I and the golden queen were plighted lovers. I know not how it first came about; I do not remember what we said to each other, and I do not remember how many days went by until I took her in my arms and told her she was all the world to me. I only know that she placed her soft arms about my neck, and that it was natural that we two should love each other,— as natural as it is for the flowers to bloom in the light of the sun. I loved that beautiful woman with a love such as few men know. She was a recluse, ignorant of the very existence of the world, the queen of a savage race of barbarians; but her soul was as pure as her face was beautiful, and when her arms were clasped about me, and her lips pressed to mine, I knew a happiness that few men know this side of heaven. Ah, *querida hermosa mia*, the memory of you makes me at once as happy as an archangel in the highest heaven and as miserable as the lost souls who writhe in endless torment!

"For three months I remained immured in the palace of the golden queen, three months that sped by as an hour, and then I was seized with the desire to go from that place and take my loved one with me, and I set about devising a way to leave the city of the accursed Caribs. No one ever disturbed us, for the people were not allowed to go near the queen, and we might have been there until now but for my desire to go again among my own people and be joined in wedlock to her I loved. We are fools in this world, Señor; such fools that we would flee from paradise as did our common parents of Eden.

"To make our escape we arranged in this wise: The queen called the priest to her and told him that the great spirits had blessed her people with bountiful harvests, and to celebrate this it was her desire that all the people, old and young, go four days' march into the forest and hold a feast and a great dance. When they were gone we intended to escape. The priest said he would send the people, but he himself was not allowed to go more than an hour's march from the city, as it was his duty to watch over the gates and the palace of the queen. The queen then commanded that he should go with the people. He steadfastly refused, saying that his religion was above even his queen; and we had to be content with that.

"When we knew the people had gone, we stole out of the palace to go to the gate of the city. It was a glad sight to me to see the look of great wonder that came over her face when for the first time in her life my beautiful queen looked upon the sky and the trees and the outer world. She took my hand in hers, and we went like two children going out to play in the meadows. Just before we reached the city gate that accursed priest saw us and came running after us with a bow and arrows in his hands. He shot an arrow at me, and it struck my arm. The arrow was poisoned, and the poison seemed like molten fire running in my veins. It almost maddened me with pain, but I grasped the hand of the queen and sped on desperately, for I was running for my life and for all that life held dear to me. This priest was a young man, and could run like a wild deer, and before we reached the swamp he overtook us and struck me with a stone knife. See, here is the scar he made. My poisoned arm was swollen and useless, but with my other hand I drew my revolver and shot at the priest, slightly wounding him in the shoulder. He seemed to be a man crazed, which I think was because I was carrying away his queen, and there was no fear about him. He seemed to have the strength of a giant, and he grasped me by the throat, threw me to the ground, and took my revolver from me. He had seen me shoot, knew how to use the weapon, and as I lay stunned and half fainting on the ground he pointed it at my heart. Just as he fired the queen threw herself forward to defend me, the bullet intended for me entered her bosom, her crimson life blood spurted in my face, and she fell dying in my arms. The priest drew back in fear at what he had done, and I forgot him for the time in my grief for my loved one. Oh, God! I can see her now, her beautiful face upturned to me in her agony of death. She whispered to me that she would love me in the other world as in this, and then she was dead. The memory of her dying face has haunted me from that hour to this, and will haunt me until I close my eyes in death.

"Do you know what madness is? I felt madness when my beloved queen died in my arms. The blood roared in my brain with a noise like the roaring of an angry sea, the sky seemed red, and my strength grew until I had the strength of twenty demons. I grasped that heathen priest by the throat, I tore his very flesh apart, I crushed the bones in his body, and then I wailed because he was dead and beyond my power to harm him further.

"Then sadness and grief came upon me like a cloud. I caressed the dead form of my loved one, I opened her beautiful eyes that were already glazed with death, I besought her to speak, and I prayed that I might be allowed to die with her. But she was dead; her pure soul had gone to a better world than this, and all that was left me was to return her body to the earth. I buried her there by the edge of the swamp, and then I plunged once more into the wilderness, and left that accursed place where I had known more than the gladness of life and worse than the bitterness of death.

"When at last I found my way again to Mexico I found my father upon his bed of death. He took my hand in his, told me greatness was mine if I would take it, and then he closed his eyes forever. I had no taste for honors or

"When I wander in the desert, sometimes she comes to me."

glory, my ambition was buried in that cruel grave by the morass in Yucatan, and I became what I now am—a wanderer upon the face of the earth, one with no joy in living, a saddened and heart-broken man, longing for the day of my death.

"Long ago my friends all deserted me. They say I am crazy—I, who might bear one of the honored names of this land if I would not wander like a wild man in the deserts and on the border. They are the deceived ones, not I. I have known the fulness of life, and I know that happiness is not in empty honors and the cheers of multitudes of fools. And when I wander in the desert, sometimes she comes to me, she, my loved one. It is not her memory that comes, it is she herself. Many times in the darkness I can see her beautiful eyes beaming upon me, I can feel the sweep of her golden hair above my face, I can feel the deep joy of her presence. Ah, she comes now, she comes now! Do you not see? Is she not beautiful? Oh, *querida, amante,* darling, come nearer; touch me; speak to me!"

The man fell forward upon his face, a white froth gathered at his mouth, and there was such an expression in his eyes as I never saw before. I feared that he was dying and I hurried away to find help to carry him to a house and care for him. I met an officer of the barracks strolling along, and I tried to get him to hurry to the man. No man hurries in Mexico, and the officer sauntered along like one who had eternity before him. When we came to the prostrate man the officer looked at him a moment, and then, as he rolled a brown cigarette between his fingers, he turned to me and said:

"Do not fear, Señor. He will recover soon. It is only Pablo Garcia, the crazed one, and he is often thus."

THE HERALD OF
THE GREAT WHITE CHRIST

THE HERALD OF THE GREAT WHITE CHRIST

F chronicles had been written of all the strange things that came to pass in the olden time in the Southwest, we would know many tales that are now lost to us forever. Races that once flourished there are now faded from the face of the earth and forgotten among men. Chiefs and priests and leaders have vanished with their nations, and left no records for those who came after them. But sometimes a tale escapes the blight of change and forgetfulness, and comes down to us freighted with the joys and sorrows of men who have long since returned to the dust. To two sources do we owe the tale of Casca, the exile, the first herald who bore tidings of the Christ to the nation he discovered in the wilds of an unknown country. The records left by Vasquez de Coronado tell a

little of his strange story; and high up on the side of a frowning cliff in the Grand Cañon of the Rio Colorado, there are words in the Spanish language, chiseled in the living rock, that tell more of Francisco Casca. Some of the stone letters and words have been obliterated by the ravages of time and the elements, but from what remain, this meagre tale has been pieced out. It is but a simple tale, and is best fitted by simple language; but it has a certain interest as being a record wrested from that silent, brooding, desert land of the old Southwest.

In the year of our Lord 1540, a band of valiant Christian soldiers set out to conquer the mysterious land of Cibola, to bring the inhabitants of its far-famed seven cities under the sway of the king of Spain, and to plant the holy faith of the Great White Christ among the red heathen who dwelt in that part of New Granada that was dedicated to the holy patron, Saint Francis. Vasquez Coronado was the chief, and with him he took fifteen hundred men, besides a thousand horses, a herd of cattle, and a drove of sheep. The army was richly furnished with silken trappings, burnished

armor, deadly guns and swords, and instruments of music. Priests were with the cavalcade,
for the expedition was called a crusade of con-
version; but the rank and file of the praying
conquistadores were lured on by visions of the
rich pillage they would loot in the walled cities
of Cibola, more than by zeal for spreading the
creed of the Christ.

Among the common soldiers was one young
man, Francisco Casca, who cared more to save
the darkened souls of the heathen than for the
treasures that might be found in their land.

A quiet man was Don Francisco Casca, who
prayed much and talked but little; and he was
not liked by the rollicking, swearing, reckless,
ambitious soldiers of the cavalcade.

The expedition of Coronado was a brave
crusade, and the echoes of its wonders and
glories are still heard in the history of the
Spanish Southwest. But before the end of the
campaign, under the tattered silken trappings
of the weary *conquistadores*, there beat many
disappointed hearts; for the famed priceless
jewels of Cibola proved to be only worthless
turquoise stones; the wealth of the land was a
myth, and even the holy cause of the Faith

fared illy, for the dark heathen were tenacious of the worship of their own unhallowed gods. Often the adventurers hungered for food, often they were mad with thirst, and many and deep were the curses they cast upon the land of Cibola. The soldiers grew morose and sullen, and were fierce and unmerciful in their treatment of the Indians they met on the plains and in the deserts; and many men lost hope of ever setting foot again upon the genial soil of sunny Spain. Coronado sought much and found little, less even than did Francisco Casca, who was banished from his fellows in the early days of the expedition.

When the campaign was yet young, after a tedious march across a desert of sand, the cavalcade encamped by the river of the brute Indians of Yuma, and the men were suffering so much from burning thirst that many of them threw themselves flat upon the banks and drank from the river like beasts. They remained in this camp for many days, refusing to go farther, for they believed that the land was under a curse, and that the Indians were the children of the devil. And when, one day, an Indian came toward the camp, he was shot down by a sullen soldier. The soldier was not punished by the commander nor censured by the priests. Nor was the Indian buried; he was left on the sands to rot.

The priests were indifferent to the killing of the Indian; the commander paid no heed whatever; the soldiers laughed and praised the one who shot him. But Francisco Casca protested that the deed was a sin, and a cowardly act. His protests stirred bad blood, and the men cursed him for a coward and a chicken-hearted woman, and one burly soldier struck him on the head with a staff. Casca was a brave man, even though he lacked bluster and bravado, and with his naked fists he chastised the man who had struck him until the man lost consciousness. Then the enemies of Casca seized and bound him, and took him a prisoner to the tent of Coronado.

The chief was sulking in his tent, sick at heart over the bad plight of his expedition. He liked not to be disturbed because of the fights of unruly soldiers. The men preferred the charge against Casca. They swore that he was in the wrong, that he had instigated the brawl, and that in behalf of a brute Indian he had humiliated and almost killed one of the bravest and best men of the company. Casca endeavored to speak in his own behalf, but was angrily interrupted by his chief.

"By the holy Saint Francis! I would rather kill every heathen in all Cibola than that harm should be done to as good a man as you have assaulted," said Coronado, frowning darkly upon the prisoner. "And I am somewhat minded to deal to you the same portion that was dealt to the dog of an Indian. Through all the campaign you have prayed when you should have fought, and you have cooled the ardor of my soldiers by the cant you have always preached about saving the souls of the pagan brutes who dwell in this accursed land. Should we succeed in reaching the Seven Walled Cities, I believe you would desert us and join in with the Cibolans, should they prove to be the stronger. I like not your drivel and your cant, and I deem you unfit to be a member of the army. You love these brutish Indians better than you love the men of your own blood; and, in punishment for your insubordination, I decree that you be discharged from my company, without pay and without honor. Señor Castenada," calling his secretary, "strike the name of Francisco Casca from the roll of our numbers, write him down as lost in the desert, and let not his name be written again in the records of our adventures.

"Francisco Casca, rebel that you are, I have shown you mercy in not ordering you to be shot or hanged. Now go from my camp. Dwell if you will among the unbaptized heathen, and if you are seen again by any man of mine, he has my leave to shoot you down as he would shoot a wolf. Now go!"

And thus Francisco Casca went forth from his fellows, an exile, into the desert, to find what fare would be his among the unknown people of that undiscovered country. And as he went his eyes were filled with tears, and his thoughts turned in longing to the vine-clad hills of his village home in Spain, the home his eyes should never rest upon again in his life.

As Casca went forth into the desert he carried his gun, a bag of food and a skin of water; but he was not allowed to take his horse. The land he was in was an absolute solitude; the only vegetation was the scant bushes of the chapparel, and the trees of a kind of high cactus that stood up like sentinels

guarding the desert. The shifting sands of the
desert ran in waves like the billows of the sea,
the heat of the sun was deadening, and there
was no shade of any kind. At night he lay
down on the bare plain to sleep, and the wail-
ing of the hungry coyotes sounded to him like
the voices of lost souls. Thus for seven days
wandered Francisco Casca, the exile; faint,
thirsty and hungry by day; lonely, desolate
and sorrowful by night. And after the seventh
day there was no more food in his bag, no more
water in the skin, and he was sick, foot-sore
and weary, and lost in the cruel, deserted land
of sand that, save him, had no inhabitants but
reptiles and wild beasts.

For two days after his food was exhausted,
Casca wandered on, stumbling blindly from
weakness, and often falling in the sand. He
was now in a great cañon with towering
mesa walls, and through the cañon ran the bed
of a stream. But there was no water. When
he had been two days without food or drink, his
tongue was swollen until it hung from his
mouth; his eyes were dry and bloodshot; his
lips were parched, and his strength was so little
that scarce could he place one foot beyond the

" But there was no water."

other. Forgotten were his home and loved ones in sunny Andalusia; forgotten were the enemies in the camp of Coronado, and all the longing of his soul was for water. At last the remnant of his strength was gone; his knees trembled, and he fell prone upon the sand.

"Water, merciful God, or I die!" he moaned.

Did the saints hear his prayer? Was not that water just beyond?

With the strength born of new hope he rises from his swoon; his limbs are strong again; he leaps and runs toward the lake of blessed water. The lake spreads miles wide before him; the sunlight glints upon its waves, and cool breezes blow from its clear surface and fan his heated brow.

"Oh, thank God, thank God, for water!" and he rushes to meet the lapping waves, rushes and throws himself headlong into the water to drink his fill and bathe his burning body. The roar of the waves makes glad music to his ears, the sheen of the water is a beautiful picture to his eyes, and he opens wide his lips to drink in the blessed draught that God has sent him—and then the cruel mirage fades from his bewitched sight. He finds he is lying prone upon his face, and his mouth is filled with the accursed hot sand of the pitiless desert!

It was a mirage; and as it faded from his vision the light of reason faded from his eyes, and he fell, swooning, to die like a famished beast in the trackless wilds of the desert.

In a time so old that history knows it not, the land of the North, where the tall mountains are, and the land that lies by the ocean of the rising sun, were inhabited by nations of people, who tilled the soil and dwelt in towns, and who worshipped the mighty gods that dwelt in the sun. These nations flourished and waxed great in numbers and prospered, until there came an evil time when hordes of savages came down upon them and drove them away from the lands that were theirs. Then they journeyed to the southward and to the westward, building mounds as they went, and filling the mounds with offerings to their gods. And the gods led them to the safety of a silent land that was hedged about with wildernesses and desolate places; and in this land they builded towns and planted fields, and for many generations were secure from the ravages of savage enemies. It was the custom of these nations to live in remote communities called pueblos; and the people of each pueblo, in time, came to care but little for their kinsmen who dwelt in other pueblos. These were the people who are believed by some to have been the ancestral stock of all the tribes and nations of American Indians : an unanswerable enigma to the scientists, who know not if they sprang from the Mayas, or the Aztecs, or the Toltecs, or from the savage tribes of the roaming Indians of the North, or whether they are descended from Mongolians, who drifted with storms to America. Some conjecture that they were the parent race of the semi-civilized nations that dwelt in the valley of Anahuac; others believe that they were off-shoots from the Anahuac nations, and to this day they remain as they were found by Coronado—the unanswerable riddle that scientists have been trying to guess for almost four hundred years.

In one of the larger of the old pueblos there dwelt a priest who desired to found a new pueblo, and, with a few hundred of his people, he journeyed until he came to a small valley, where water always flowed and where the grass was

thick and green. And in this valley they builded
the holy estufa, and lighted the undying fire.
The women built houses and the men planted
fields; and they named the place the Pueblo of the
Strangers, for they were strangers in a strange
land who had founded it. It was but seldom
that wayfarers came to this pueblo, for it was
located in a remote place, and its people saw
but few besides those of their own nation. The
gods smiled upon them; their crops were bountiful; their numbers increased with the passing
seasons; their hunters were successful in the
chase, and they were a happy people.

When the Pueblo of the Strangers was many
generations old, it was ruled over by a wise
chief whose name was Es-Tah; and he had a
daughter named Lo-Eetah, who was more
beautiful than any other woman in all the
Pueblo nations. Many men of her nation
sought Lo-Eetah for wife, but she smiled upon
none, and seemed to care for no man. Many
of the men were sorrowful because of this, and
some of them said bitterly that Lo-Eetah must
expect the gods to send her a husband from
above, as she seemed to think no man she had
ever seen was good enough for her. But, though

the young men pleaded and her father urged, Lo-Eetah refused to wed, and she herself did not know why.

One day Lo-Eetah went alone to the western mesa to gather berries. She liked to go alone, for the jabbering and gossip of the other women tired her; and she liked to gaze away across the plains and mountains and deserts, and wonder what lands and peoples there were at the place where the sun comes up, and at the place where the sun goes down. On this day Lo-Eetah, busy with thinking, wandered farther than was her wont, and in the heat of the day she found that she had reached the farthest edge of the mesa and was many miles from home.

"I must return soon" she thought, "else my father will think I have been borne away by the Navajos."

But to rest herself before returning she sat down upon a rock, and looked away over the valley that lay before her. Before she had looked long she started up in affright, for coming toward her was a strangely clad man, who ran and staggered through the sand. He seemed different from any man she had ever seen; but she feared he was a Navajo, disguised, who sought to capture her for a slave, and she hid herself behind a clump of cactus to see what he would do. The man ran wildly, one way and then another, and at last fell forward upon his face and moved no more.

The maiden knew not what to do, and for a long time she sat and watched the silent figure lying so still upon the sand. The man lay so motionless that Lo-Eetah thought he must be dead; but to guard against a ruse she drew her bone knife, climbed down the side of the mesa, and cautiously stole up to the quiet figure. At last she reached the man and stood over him in wonder, for the face she looked upon was a white face, and the garments he wore were different from any she had ever seen.

She examined the man to learn if he were dead, and found that he yet lived; so she knew that he had fainted from thirst. She opened her skin of water, dashed some in his face, and forced some between his parched lips. After a long time the man opened his eyes; then he sat up and gazed at her in wonder, and then he seized her water-skin and drank all the liquid that remained. When he had finished drinking he spoke to the maid in a tongue which she could not understand, nor could he understand her speech. She gave him her basket of berries, and he ate of them ravenously, like a starving beast. When he had eaten them all, he took the hand of the maid in his and smiled upon her. And in return she smiled upon him, for never before had she seen so handsome a man, nor a man with a white skin.

Thus was the prayer of Francisco Casca answered, and thus was he miraculously saved from perishing like a beast in the desert.

Francisco Casca was a virile man of great endurance, and his strength soon returned to him after he had partaken of the water and berries given him by Lo-Eetah. His hunger and thirst satisfied, he made a critical examination of his strange companion. She did not grow restive under his scrutiny, for she was also examining him. He saw before him a comely, well-formed maid, with rounded figure, jet-black hair and soft, dark eyes. A necklace of silver and turquoise was about her neck, silver rings were on her fingers, silver circlets on her wrists, and her kirtle was fastened by buttons of bone and silver. Over her head she wore a bright-

colored rebosa, of native weaving; her body
was covered with a kirtle, fastened at the side,
and falling to her knees; her feet were encased
in moccasins; her ankles were wound round
with long strips of fine, white buckskin, and a
buckskin belt was around her waist. In her
hand she bore a basket of willow-ware, in which
she had carried the berries she had gathered,
and by her side lay the empty water-skin, which
was made from the tanned hide of the buffalo.

The maiden smiled upon him, for she liked
his face, and was not afraid, although she did
not know whether he was a human or an immortal.

At the time of Casca's exile from the company, the *conquistadores* had encountered none
but the nomad Indians, and when Casca saw
this maid, he thought:

"This is no Apache or brute Yuma Indian.
Surely I must now be in the land of Cibola, and
this must be a daughter of that people."

"Maid," said he, "of what people are you?"

But Lo-Eetah could not understand him,
and they were forced to converse by signs. It
was a difficult way to communicate with each
other, but they made shift to impart some intel-

ligence; and Casca learned that the maid belonged to a tribe that dwelt but a few hours'
march to the east, that her people did not like
unknown men, and that it would not be safe
for him to go among them until he could tell
them of himself.

Lo-Eetah then conducted her strange guest
to a cave in the side of the mesa, that was used
as a shelter by hunters of her pueblo. By signs
she told him that she would go home, but with
the coming of the sun on the morrow she
would return, and bring food and water.
Casca's fear of the terrors of the desert was so
great that he was minded to go with her, and
brave what dangers there might be; but this
Lo-Eetah would in no wise permit.

When she started away, the fear of the
solitude of the wilderness came upon him again,
and he called her back by shouting. She returned and stood mutely before him, as if to
inquire what he might want. Again he essayed
to go with her, but she dissuaded him by making
signs, indicating that by so doing he would
place his life in danger.

"If this maid fails to return," mused Casca,
"then will my life be lost anyhow. But I think

she is honest, for such eyes as her's cannot look lies. She is comely, too; and I feel that I have known her always."

Casca had been a wayfarer and a wanderer for many years. The pleasures of home and the love of women were only memories with him, and it is not strange that he fell in love with the child of nature who came to him so providentially in the desert. Acting upon a sudden impulse he took the face of the Indian girl between his hands and kissed her. The face of Lo-Eetah lighted up with a radiant smile, she breathed reverently upon Casca's hands, and then she turned and sped swiftly away across the bare, brown mesa.

Casca stood motionless, watching her receding figure. A smile was on his face, and in his heart was a greater feeling of content than he had known for many weary months. Lo-Eetah turned once and waved her hand to him, and then sped on; and as she ran, never had the world seemed so fair to her,—never had life seemed so sweet as since she had met the white-skinned wanderer in the sand valley by the western mesa.

A strange wooing. They, strangers, people

of different worlds, stood in the fading light of the setting sun, and mutely, silently pledged each other in love. They could not speak to each other in the languages of the tongue, but they spoke eloquently in the language of the heart.

Francisco Casca stood in the dim twilight, gazing after the receding form of the one who was all the world to him. He was destitute, lost in the forbidding solitudes of a land of barbarians, a wandering outcast, exiled from his people; beyond him lay an unknown and undiscovered country, filled with he knew not what hordes of savages and what measure of suffering. But the one great hour of existence had come to him; he had found the soul's desire, and a love-song of Castile sprang to his lips as he turned to enter the cave to rest.

Lo-Eetah came with the sun of the morning, bringing fresh water, meat of deer, and maize cakes of her own making. She kissed Casca, breathed upon his hands, and sat smiling while he ate. When he had finished, she gave him a roll of tobacco to smoke, and then set about the arduous task of teaching him her language. She pointed to herself and said " Lo-Eetah." Then she pointed in turn to the water, the

various articles of food, the sky, the sun, and
every other thing within sight, and as she
pointed to each one she spoke the name it was
known by in the language of her nation. Casca
learned rapidly; and thus they passed the time
until the sun was sinking in the west, and then
Lo-Eetah went again to her home.   Her daily
absence caused no comment among her people,
for she was a strange maid and did as her own
will bade her.

Every day she carried food to the cave in
the side of the mesa; each day she spent
long hours in teaching Casca the speech of her
people; and there came a time when he could
talk well in the language she had taught him.

"Now, O sweet stranger," she said to him
one day, "tell me of yourself.   Are you an outcast god, thrown down from the sun to fall in
the valley where I found you; or are you a man
from a nation of the people of the earth?"

"No god am I," said Casca, "although I
am an outcast.   I am a man of Spain, a great
land that lies far, far to the east—far to the
east of a great water called the ocean."

"I have heard tales of that water," mused
Lo-Eetah, "and the old men tell that once our

fathers of long ago dwelt by the noise of its waves."

Then Casca told her of the army of white men who were wandering somewhere in the land of Cibola, and of his exile from them. Then he told of the Christ, whose servant he was, of his goodness and mercy; that he was the ruler of the world; that he was the son of the one true God, and that she, also, was one of his children. The maid believed, listening in joy and wonder; for was it not her lover who told her? and must it not, therefore, be true? Casca took water and baptized the maid in the holy faith, and then together they went across the plains toward the Pueblo of the Strangers.

When they came near the pueblo they met men going to the fields to labor. The men took fright at the strange white man, and ran back to the pueblo to sound the alarm and call out the chief priest. When Casca and Lo-Eetah came to the gate in the wall of the pueblo, old Es-tah came forth, bearing the symbols of his office, to ask who this man might be. The chief's mind was troubled because the stranger came with his daughter,—for he feared witchcraft. He waved his hand and called out:

"Daughter, who is this strange man, with a white skin and strange garb, whom you bring thus to the pueblo of your people?"

The crowd stood motionless to hear, and Lo-Eetah looked proudly from her father to Casca as she replied:

"He who comes with me, O, my father, is the Herald of the Great White Christ!"

Casca stepped forward, uncovered his head, and, speaking loudly so all might hear, said:

"I am a wanderer, come from a great nation of white men who dwell beyond the sea. I am come to you as the herald of the undying King, the white Christ of the true believers. I am come to tell you that you are the children of this Christ, and to teach you the truth, which is immutable and unchangeable."

The chief priest and the people wondered much who this great white Christ could be, and they asked many questions. And when they learned that this wanderer declared that their own gods were false, and that only his God was true, many angry murmurs were heard, and Casca was in danger. Then Lo-Eetah, seeing his peril, stepped to his side, placed her hand in his, and said:

"Oh, you people of sudden anger, hear me, Lo-Eetah, the child of the chief priest! I am to be the wife of this white-skinned wanderer, and he speaks truth to you, and I believe in the great Christ of whom he tells you."

Then turning to her father, who stood mute with wonder, she said:

"Father, the stranger is weak and ill. Shelter him and feed him, and tell the people to go to their homes, and on another day they can meet in the open ground and hear the stranger tell of the new creed."

Es-tah loved his daughter, and he did as she wished. And as the people went toward their homes they wondered much.

"How comes he to speak in our speech?" asked one. "Where was he made known to Lo-Eetah?" others asked; and some wondered if he were an immortal, and others questioned if he had been sent from the sky to be husband to Lo-Eetah. So there was much wonder in the pueblo, and also much fear; for the people liked not the talk of an unknown god, and they feared the anger of their own gods might fall heavily upon them because of the presence of this mysterious herald.

The pueblo Indians have been a hospitable people in all ages, and until it should be fully decided whether the wayfarer were friend or enemy, he would receive the treatment accorded to an honored guest. The place where Casca had been stopped, and where he had spoken to the people, was just outside the walls of the pueblo. As he turned to lead his guest within the walls, old Es-tah's heart was troubled, for he feared he might be doing grievous wrong in harboring this wanderer from an unheard-of race, who said so boldly that the ancient gods of the pueblos were false gods. Never before had he seen a man with a white skin, and he feared somewhat that this strange being might be a witch who had assumed the form of a man in order to win favor among the people, and then work evil upon them. But he led the way to his own house, nor did he speak a single word. And Lo-Eetah walked proudly by the side of the white stranger who was to be her husband.

Casca looked wonderingly about him at the strange houses of the Cibolans. The houses were built of adobe and stone, were terraced and all joined together, and some of them

" He led the way to his own house nor did he speak."

were six stories high. There were no doors or windows in the lower stories, and entrance was gained by climbing ladders and then descending through the roofs. On the housetops wild fruits were drying, strips of meat were curing in the sun, and men and women sat on the walls, engaged in weaving fabrics, and in molding and decorating pottery. The people looked shyly at Casca as he passed, and those who were occupied ceased from their toil.

"Surely," thought Casca, "here is rich soil for the seed of the word of God; for people who are weavers of fabrics and builders of tall houses must be of reasoning minds, and with such people the mighty truth must prevail."

Es-tah led the way up a ladder and into a large room, where some members of his family were sitting.

"Leave me alone with the stranger," said he. And his people quietly went away, even Lo-Eetah going with them.

When they were alone the priest examined Casca carefully, scrutinizing his garments, and even feeling of his skin to make sure it was not a mask. When he had examined him he said:

"Now tell me of yourself, and of this white Christ, whose herald you say you are."

Casca told the story of his wandering from his native land, of being driven an exile from the company of the Spaniards, and of the love for God and the love for his fellow-men that had impelled him to journey across the world to spread the true gospel of the holy faith.

" Will the white Christ, your master, also come to the pueblo of my people?" asked the priest.

"The Christ dwells in the sky," replied Casca, devoutly crossing himself, " and he journeys not upon the earth in his visible person. But his presence is everywhere, and he guards his children like a loving father, wheresoever they may wander."·

" How can you prove this?" asked Es-tah.

" He saved me from death in the desert. I was alone in a solitude, lost in a desolate land, and he guided me to safety."

The priest wore an earnest look, and he bowed his head in thought. And then Casca told him all the tale of the Christ, of his pilgrimage upon the earth, of his suffering, and of his divine compassion. When he had finished

"Casca told him all the tale of the Christ."

darkness was falling upon the pueblo, for he loved his theme and had spoken long.

The priest took Casca's hand and said:

"Stranger, the tale you have told is a wondrous tale, and you might not tell it to many men of my race and live; for the men of my race will kill if they think a man blaspheme our gods. I am the chief priest of this nation. Many long days and nights have I fasted, seeking after the pure truth; but I say to you that often have I been troubled because the truth came not to me, and I have thought that there must be greater gods than those that were known to my fathers. I believe that you have spoken in true words, for there is no doubt in your mind. And, too, the wisest priests of my fathers knew that a God of Love dwelt in the sky and it may be that the old god of my people is one with the white Christ you worship. I am an old man and I know much wisdom, but I have known little of this God of Love. I dwell in this remote pueblo, and the knowledge of this god is secret knowledge that may only be spoken to priests of the highest class. I am of that class now, but since I have learned the greatest of the mysteries there has been no other priest near to teach me of this god. Now I will retire to a place apart and will meditate, and if in my wisdom I find that your speech is truth, I will go with you among my people to teach them of this unknown Christ."

Es-tah gathered his robes about him and retired to a secret room, and for four days he was not seen again. After he had gone the women placed food before Casca, and conducted themselves as though he were the master of the house and they his servants.

"Oh, haughty Coronado," said Casca in his native tongue, "ride on in your ruthless march of rapine! I will abide among the simple people of this isolated place and teach them of the Christ, the Holy Virgin and the saints. I will teach them, too, that love of man which is the foundation for the love of God. My name will be forgotten and yours will emblazon the pages of history, but in the blest book of life the name of the lowly exile shall lead that of the haughty conqueror."

For four days Casca lived a quiet life, going among the people of the pueblo, talking to them in their own language, learning of their ways of life and their channels of thought.

On the morning of the fifth day old Es-tah came forth from his fast with a happy look upon his face. He told Casca that during his fast a vision had been revealed to him, that the gates of the white man's heaven had been opened to the eyes of his soul, and that he knew the creed of the white Christ to be the one true creed.

Then Casca and the old priest went among the people preaching the creed' of the Christ. Some of the people were affrighted, some were troubled, some received the missionaries with dark looks of scorn, yet many believed and were baptized. The doubting ones demanded proof, and as reason would not suffice, Casca took his gun and killed a wolf that was running on the mesa a long distance away. He believed he might be forgiven for deceiving men into believing the truth. And the people marvelled much, and said :

" This man takes into his hands a stick, and lo, it sends fire to a great distance and kills with a noise ! Surely he is the servant of a god, and the words he speaks to us must be true words."

Yet the habit of the old worship was strong upon them, and it was many years before the last one laid down the belief in the gods of his fathers and called himself a child of the new Christ. Some of the old men even died in the old worship. But Casca was yet a young man when all the people of that nation held the cross as the emblem of their faith.

The oaths of the priesthood were taken by an Indian, and Casca was wedded to Lo-Eetah in the form prescribed by the church.

The *conquistadores* never came to the Pueblo of the Strangers, and no man of Spanish blood ever knew the fate of Francisco Casca.

In after years the yoke of slavery was placed upon the Pueblo tribes. These people rose in revolt; bloody battles were fought and the war was carried even to the isolated place where stood the Pueblo of the Strangers. Casca, Lo-Eetah his wife, and Estah the priest, had gone, long before, to the land beyond the sunrise; but their descendants, and all the people of the pueblo, fought against the enslavers, whom they called false Christians because of their cruelty. The people of this pueblo were few in numbers, and in a fierce battle they, men, women and children, were swept from the earth, and their homes became the hiding places of wild beasts.

Years, decades and centuries have rolled by; the war of the Pueblos is long past; the yoke of slavery is an almost forgotten thing, and the land that once was Cibola is filling with hordes of white-faced people from the East. The Pueblo of the Strangers has returned to dust, its forgotten people have no records in the history known to the new dwellers in the land; and, but for a record cut in undying rock, they, and the herald who went to them with tidings of the white Christ, would be known of no more upon the earth.

High up on the side of a frowning cliff in the Grand Cañon of the Rio Colorado, there are words, chiseled in the face of the solid rock. The words are in the Spanish language, and if they are translated they will be found to read thus:

"I have reached the sundown time of life; my days to live are few, and this record cut in living stone will be the last work I shall do upon the earth. I am a Christian and a man of Spain, and my name is Francisco Casca. My wife is dead and my life is lonely, yet have my years been happy years, for in this stranger-land I have learned the fullness of the knowledge that

God is everywhere, and that His love is a love that passeth all understanding. This is my last work before I die, and here I write down the true account——"

What need to read it further? For what was chiseled upon the rock is the same as the tale that is written here.

THE LAST MAN OF A NATION

THE LAST MAN OF A NATION

I AM an old man, and my blood flows slowly and my limbs are weary with the weariness of age. The bones of my people lie crumbling in the dust, and I, the last man of the people of this pueblo, am waiting here alone until the time shall come when I shall be called to join my people in the houses of our Fathers in the sun. When I die the sacred fires in the estufa will die, and the people of the Pueblo of the Exiles will be no more upon the face of the earth, for I am the last man of my nation.

When the noise of your footsteps first broke the silence of this pueblo, I loved you not, for you are a white-skinned man and are of the race who live in the North, and seek after new things. But my heart has been lonely here among the crumbling houses of my vanished people, and you have been good to

95

me, an old man and a stranger to you. So I call you my friend, and I will tell you of the people of the Pueblo of the Exiles. When I have told you, then take your sticks and papers that talk, and go to your own people; for the weakness of death is stealing through my veins and in his last days it is not good that a Priest of the Sun should be with a man of another blood. And, moreover, I care not, henceforth, to look upon the face of my fellow-men. I have been alone in my sad and bitter old age until I have a desire for loneliness. I will lay me down to die where none shall see me.

I was born in this pueblo, in this house, and in this very room where I hold speech with you. That was more than eighty years in the past, and even then my nation numbered but a very few. My birth was hailed with great joy, and a feast and a great dance were given; for the blood that flowed in my veins was the blood of priests, and I was entitled to become a Priest of the Bow, which was the highest of the orders of the priesthood among the people. All my life I have been a priest and a chief, and have followed the wisdom that was passed down from the Fathers.

In the far time of the past the forefathers of my nation belonged to one of the greatest nations of all the Pueblo Indians, and the old tales tell that at first they came to this land from a rich land that lies far toward the great ocean of the rising sun. After the nation had builded a great pueblo, and had lived long in the land that lies not far to the east from here, there was born to a woman of our clan a female child of wondrous beauty. Her beauty was greater than had ever been seen by my people before, and the medicine chiefs blessed her and said she was a child who was dear to Those Above. In her ways she was also beautiful, and she had a knowledge and a wisdom beyond her years.

She was named La-Lah-Koitza, and when she had grown from a child to be a woman, her great beauty had grown also until it was like the beauty of the sun; and the priests and the chiefs of the clans sought her for a wife, and they stayed near her to see her and to hear her speech. For love of her the men forsook the work in the fields, and some of the priests almost forgot the worship in the estufas; and because of this the wise ones among the old men were grieved, for they knew that the love of her was already beginning to cause men to hate their brothers, and they feared that when she made her choice of a husband there would be such hatred among the other men of the tribe that murder might be done.

The maid was wise, and to hold peace in the nation she at first held aloof from all men, until it seemed that she would be the wife of no man. The old men were also grieved by this, for a woman should be a wife, and they could not judge whether it were best for the maid to wed or not. But the heart of the maid decided,—for her heart was as the heart of all maids, whether their skin be dark or white,—and in time it turned in love to a man.

The man she loved was a man of no renown. He belonged to a clan of poor people, and he never gave her presents as the others did; but he was dear to her, and she became his wife. When she was wed the young chiefs who had sought her sulked in silence and with dark faces. One great chief who had sought her declared revenge upon her and upon the man who had taken her for wife, and he said that La-Lah-Koitza, the beautiful woman, was a witch.

Then it came about that the waters in the pools became defiled, and the maize plants in the fields were pulled up by the roots in the time of night ; and the angry chief said it was the work of La-Lah-Koitza, the beautiful witch. But the man who said it, although he was a chief and a priest, was a liar; and if he had been even a god, instead of a priest, I would say he was a liar, for he did the things himself, so that he might call La-Lah-Koitza a witch and work his hatred upon her.

Then the times of the pueblo were full of trouble and the old men prayed daily in the estufas. Many of the people thought the beautiful woman not a witch, but a good woman ; and because of these things it seemed that war would come among the people of the pueblo, and a war among the men of one people is not good in the sight of Those Above. Many angry words were spoken of this matter, but the wicked men had their way. The terrible dance of the great-knife was ordered, and La-Lah-Koitza was doomed to die the awful death that the laws and customs of our fathers bid us inflict upon her who was found to be a witch.

The men of the tribe of the beautiful woman

were mad with anger and sorrow, and they
made ready to make war for her; but La-Lah-
Koitza was a wise woman, and she knew that
such a war was not good. So she called the
clan to meet in a desert place in the dead time
of the night, and she spoke to them and said it
would be good to go away to a far land and
build a new pueblo; there to live in peace, and
make no war upon the other clans of their own
nation. Her beauty was so great that the men
were charmed by it, and they listened to her
words. The anger left their hearts, the darkness went from their faces, and they said her
words were wise words. And thus it was,
that, though women have often in times past
been the cause of stirring men up to war, this
young woman of my ancestors did by her good
counsel turn away her brethren from shedding
the blood of their kinsmen in battle.

So they gathered their people about them,
and took meal, and maize, and seeds, and the
things they would need in their work; and in
silence all of that clan stole out of the pueblo in
the darkest time of the night. They wandered
for many weary days, and suffered much from
cold, and from hunger, and from thirst; they

were always in great fear that the wild
Apaches would fall upon them, kill the men,
and take the women and children for slaves.
But they were guided by Him who holds
the lines of our lives, and in time they came
to a pass in the mountains through which
it seemed men could not go, unless they had
wings wherewith they might fly over the great
and terrible crags and precipices that were on
either hand, and in front.

But these people were exiles and dared not
turn back; for behind them were the angry men
of their own nation, as well as the wild bands
of the Apaches, and with strength that was
given them by fear, they came through the pass
to this place. Because this place was hard
to reach they felt safe, and they stopped and
built this pueblo, which they named the Pueblo
of the Exiles.

Here my people lived for many generations,
building houses and estufas, tilling the fields,
weaving fabrics, molding jars, joining each
other in marriage, rearing their children, and
worshipping Those Above according to the true
worship of the Fathers. But the numbers of the
people did not increase, and disease seemed to

be with the little children as soon as they were born into the world. As the time grew older these things grew worse, and the shamans were greatly troubled because of them, for, in all things save health, Those Above seemed good to them.

When I was a young man, a priest of the Spanish nation came to our pueblo, telling of the great white God of his people, and asking us to leave the worship of the gods of the sun. I liked not his worship, but I knew him for a wise man, and I asked him what plague was upon my people that the little children died and that the men and women knew not health? He said we married in the circles of blood that were too near the blood of our own bodies; and that it was not good for people of one blood and one family to marry so often with each other.

I knew not if he spoke truth, but my own wife was the daughter of the brother of my father; and, in latter years, when our tribe had faded to a handful of people, my son took my daughter, his sister, for his wife. But one child was born to my son and daughter, and that child had white hair and white eyes, and knew

"I am left here alone with my sacred fire."

not as much as the wild beasts of the mountains. When this child was born, I knew that
the white priest had spoken in true words,—
and that it was not good to mix one blood too
often with itself in marriage.

This mixing of one blood has taken my
nation from the earth, but to this day I am
troubled of the matter; for the wisdom that has
come down from our fathers says that we must
marry, but that we must not take our wives
from the women of other people. Our tribe
was grown so small that my daughter was the
only woman my son could take for wife, unless
he took a wild woman of the Apaches, and I
would have killed him with my own hand if he
had brought such a woman to live in the pueblo
that was built by the fathers of my people.

In this way my people, already few, sickened
and died. The little children died before they
grew, and the older people died,one by one, until
all were gone but me; and my old wife was the
last one in this pueblo to close her eyes in the
sleep of death. My heart was very sad when
she was gone, for I was left a solitary man in
the land of my fathers, the last man of a vanished nation, and there was no more joy for me

in living. She was my wife when the hot blood of youth leaped through my veins; she was my wife in the wisdom of my manhood; she was my wife in the sorrow and bitterness of my old age,—and the saddest day I have known in my life was the day her hand grew cold in mine, and the light of life faded from her eyes. It was ten years in the past that I laid her body in the dust, and every day since then I have prayed our greatest gods to free me from my burden of life and let me join her and my children and my people in the houses of our Fathers in the sun.

And now you know the story of the Pueblo of the Exiles; you know that I, a sad old man, weary of life, am left here alone with my sacred fire, in this crumbling old pueblo, that you tell me was thought to be deserted by men until that day when you came upon me as I was praying in the estufa. Had not my ears waxed dull with age, so that I heard not your footsteps as you drew near, I would have hidden myself away from you, for I had not thought to look again upon the face of any man.

You are the last man I shall look upon in

life, for when you are gone never again will I come forth from the secret place of the fire that is hidden behind the estufa; and if strange men come to this silent place they will not know that a living man is in it.

You are a white-faced man and you are a heathen, but the sight of you has cheered the lonely heart of a sad old man, and when I pray to Those Above I will pray that the sunlight of your life may not be darkened by clouds. Now go your way, for I would be alone with the memories of my dead. Farewell.

IN THE CAVERNS OF ULO

IN THE CAVERNS OF ULO

ONE hot day in September I journeyed down the sandy valley of the Rio Grande del Norte. I was taking a vacation, seeking rest and such adventure as might be found by wandering in the quaint land of the old Southwest. I had started from an old Indian pueblo on a slow freight train. We saw Oriental-looking Indian women with water jars on their heads, walking from the *acequias* to their queer grout houses; oriental-looking Mexican villages with their clusters of adobe houses and the inevitable adobe church; and herds of sheep in charge of solitary herdsmen. Away in the distance the blue line of the Sandia mountains rose between us and the horizon, and at sundown the slow train pulled into the town of San Marcial. The conductor said the train would go no farther as that was the end of the division.

San Marcial is a pleasant town to a leisurely traveler. There is a good railroad hotel there whose attachés take an interest in the strangers within their gates, and whose guests are usually sociable and companionable. There are wide verandas around the hotel, and the streets of the little town are lined with shady trees. At night Mescalero Indians wrap themselves in their blankets and lie down on the ground near the hotel to sleep.

I was sitting on the hotel veranda, smoking a cigar, and watching the big yellow moon come up over the mesas, when an old Mescalero, wrapped in a gaudy Navajo blanket, came up to the veranda and looked at me curiously. I gave him a cigar and tried to talk to him. While thus engaged, a well-dressed Mexican of the better class took a seat at my side and said: "*Buenas tardes*, Señor!"

The Mexican was a genial, intelligent man, apparently about thirty-five years of age. He was anxious to be sociable, and, like all Mexicans, was very polite, but a perpetual sadness seemed to lurk under his smiles. We talked for an hour of Mexico, of the Indians, of the Southwest, and of the Garza revolution, until we came to know each other as well as men often do after years of acquaintance. When the hotel guests had retired, and we were sitting alone, looking out into the moonlit night, he asked me if I would like to hear a strange, true tale of an adventure he had had. Of course I wanted to hear it. Many of the strange tales of the Southwest are true, and many are false, and it is hard for one to choose between them; but the story told me by the Mexican is here recorded in the man's own words.

"The Señor has no doubt read something of the history of this country, and of the country of old Mexico, whose history is much the same, or was much the same until the present century. He knows of the traditions of the olden times that tell that the first people of this land came down to earth by way of the mighty mountain that is now called Pike's Peak—the mountain in whose shadow the Señor says he lives. Of course that tale of the people coming to earth in that way is a fable, but it is true that the first tribes who entered the great valley of Mexico came from the North. First came fierce tribes who knew but little more than the wild beasts, then wiser tribes who knew somewhat

.

of agriculture and working in metals; then other fierce tribes, who fought the other tribes, and so on, until there was almost ceaseless war in the valley that was then known as Anahuac. In time came the Olmecs, those shadowy people whose very history is known only by the dimmest traditions; then the Toltecs, who either faded away or were amalgamated with succeeding races; then came the great empire of the Montezumas, and then the great Conquest, and the sway of the white-skinned men. The tale I shall tell you is a tale of the present, but it also goes back, far before the time of the *Conquistadores*, or even the time of the Aztec supremacy. It is a strange tale and by many will be called a lie, but I say to you, Señor, that it is a true tale, and it tells almost all of sorrow or of joy that has been in my life.

"As you see, I am a Mexican. Of Mexicans there are many kinds: the Castilians, the peons, the pure-blooded Indians. I am a *mestizo*—a creole, you might call it. In my blood are strains of the purest Castilian Spanish, and also strains of Indian blood. When the *Conquistadores* came, many of them took wives from the native women. My first male Castil-

ian ancestor did this, taking his wife from a
small tribe known as the Ulo, of whom there
were not two hundred all told, and of whose
descendants I am the only one, except the
people of whom I shall tell you. In this way
the blood of my ancestors became mixed, and
it was mixed often after that, by marriage.
My mother seemed more Indian than Castilian,
for while she was a devout Catholic, she prac-
ticed old Ulo tribal rights in secret. My father
was a wise man for the place where he lived;
he saw to it that I was started in the way of
being educated, and then he died. My mother
died soon after my father, and when she lay on
her bed of death she sent for me and said to me:

"'My son, you may live to be an honored
man among the people of this country. And you
should, for there was a time when the Ulos,
who are your ancestors, were counted among
the rulers of this great valley, and they held
sway over tribes far more numerous than
their own. The old words that have come
down to me from my mother, and from my
mother's mother, and from all the women of
my line, tell that in an olden time the tribe of
the Ulo came to this valley from the North;

came to this valley and conquered it, although
the Ulos were but a small tribe.   They ruled in
the valley until the Toltecs came, that great
tribe whose numbers were as the numbers of
the birds of the air.   The Toltecs were con-
querers, and as the Ulos would serve no mas-
ters, they gathered together and sought out a
new land far to the southwest of this.   All
did not go, and the ones of the Ulos who remained in the valley have all faded from the
earth since the time of the Conquest—all but
you and me, and now you will be the only one.
The Ulos are the chosen people of Those Above;
they were promised that on the earth there
should always be a land for them, and that a
prophet should always dwell with them to keep
them faithful to the true creed of the olden time.
The descendants of the tribe that left the valley
are upon the earth to-day; I know not where,
but upon the earth I know they are, for so it
was promised.   When I was young, I longed to
go forth and seek out the dwelling-place of this
tribe of my people, but a woman is but a weak
thing; I loved your father, and I abode with
him.   But because of my longing to dwell
with my own people I have always cherished

memories of them; I have taught you, my only child, the language of this people, which language is now forgotten in the valley of Anahuac. And upon your arm I have placed the sacred mark of the Ulo, the writing that reads:

"'In this body flows the blood of Ulo.'

"'Now, my son, when my body has again been returned to the earth, go thou and seek the descendants of your forefathers; seek them and learn truth from them, and by dwelling among them be numbered among the chosen people of the world.'

"Then my mother died, and I was greatly impressed by what she had told me. It was true that she had taught me the language of the Ulo, and on my arm was tattooing that read as she had said. I was a young man, eager for adventure, and I desired greatly to find the dwelling place of this strange tribe. I went to the schools, to the heads of government depart-ments, to travelers—everywhere inquiring for a tribe known as the Ulo. No one knew anything of such a tribe, but as I believed the tribe ex-isted I traveled to the remote parts of Mexico, seeking it. I did not find anyone, however, who had ever heard of the tribe, and in time I almost abandoned hope of ever finding it. My desire to seek out this people was founded only on a desire for adventure, and not on account of the belief of my mother; but for all that, I was very loth to give up my hope of discovering them.

"After I had ceased to look for the Ulos, I became engaged as a minor officer upon a small ship that sailed from the port of Mazatlan up and down the west coast of Mexico. On one cruise we passed a barren coast, where high rock walls rose sheer at the water's edge, so steep that it seemed impossible for any living thing to scale them. The place had a charm for me on account of its being a locality destined apparently never to come under the control of man.

"The wall of rocky cliffs ran for several miles along the coast, and it chanced that as we were passing it I had a violent quarrel with my superior officer. In the heat of anger I struck him in the face, knocking him senseless. He was a vindictive man, and I knew that as soon as we reached a port he would have me arrested for mutiny. So I determined to escape, and some of the common sailors who were friends of mine, assisted me. I took a small boat, rigged it with both sails and oars, and provisioned it. Taking a few belongings, such as a revolver, photographic camera and a supply of tobacco, I embarked, getting safely put off before the officer could prevent. The ship sailed on down the coast, and before it was out of sight I saw the officer I had struck looking back at me through a glass. No doubt he was pleased, for it must have seemed to him that there were chances that I might never reach a place where I could land.

"I was very well content in my small boat. I always loved adventure, and I was happy as I sat in the boat and smoked, and looked out over the blue waves of the calm Pacific Ocean. I felt free from all the cares that beset men in the common walks of life, and it seemed to me that I should be content to drift forever, alone, on that beautiful expanse of water that seemed to stretch from the world to eternity.

"As I was near the rock cliffs that had excited my curiosity I determined to sail as close to them as I could. As I sailed along I noticed an opening in the cliffs that looked like the mouth of a cave. I sailed to this opening, and was greatly surprised to find that it was large

enough for my boat to enter. I took the oars
and rowed directly into the mouth of this opening, and was more surprised to find that it led
under a mass of overhanging rock into a perfect
little bay that was completely shut off from
sight of the ocean. The bay was very small,
containing an area of not more than forty acres,
and the rock walls rose sheer from it on every
side, extending upwards hundreds of feet.

"I moored the little boat to a crag of rock
and prepared to spend the night in the bay.
The next day I explored the bay, and discovered
the mouth of the cave, or passage, that led directly into the rock, on the side of the bay that
was toward the mainland. I took candles with
me to give light and set out walking to explore
this passage. It was wide enough for a carriage
to have passed through, and was about ten feet
from the floor to the roof. Water dripped from
its sides, and stalactites and stalagmites pro-
jected from the rocks. The passage was straight
for a long distance, when suddenly I left the
straight path, and plunged into a perfect maze
of passages that ran in every direction. It was
not long until I was completely lost, and I became greatly frightened.   It is not pleasant for

one to think he may have to wander alone in
tortuous, underground passages until he dies
from starvation.

"Has the Señor a match? Thank you; I
had allowed my cigar to go out.

"I wandered up and down the mazes of the
winding tunnels for long hours, probably crossing and recrossing my own path numbers of
times. When I was almost exhausted I came to
a set of rude stairs made out of rocks piled one
above another. The stairway seemed somewhat
as though it had been built by human hands,
and I wondered if some other man, lost and hopeless like myself, had built it in order that the
work might prevent him from becoming insane.
I climbed up the stairs, and found that they led
to a large platform that lay under a part of the
caverns which rose much higher than the roof of
the passages I had been in. A soft light came
into this cavern from a crevice high above my
head, and when my eyes had become accustomed
to this light, I looked around me, and the sight
that met my eyes was so strange that at first I
almost feared I had lost my reason. In all
parts of the cavern were human figures, some
seated, some reclining, some lying flat upon the

floor, some standing by rocks. At first I
thought they were figures of living humans, as
each was fully dressed, and all were in such life-
like positions; but I soon discovered that the
things before me were the bodies of dead men.
I cannot tell you the feeling of horror that ran
over me when I found myself in that ghastly
company. Every figure seemed perfect, none
seemed wasted or decayed, all were clothed, and
over the face of each one was a strange white
mask that closely fitted the face and showed the
nose, the mouth, in fact the contour of all the
features. The light that came down through
the rift in the rocks gave a weird effect to the
picture of silent death that was before me, and
the deathly silence that filled the cave was
almost unbearable.

"I tried to tear myself away from the grim
fascination of the ghastly cavern, but found
it hard to leave. Then I went close to the
bodies and examined some of them. I found
them to be clothed in garments made of buckskin, the buckskin having been oiled with some
mineral substance that prevented decay. The
bodies were mummified, each one being as hard
as flint, but every contour and feature was per-

The cavern of the dead.

fectly preserved. I tried to tear the mask from one of the faces, but could not, as the thing seemed made of iron. I did succeed, though, in tearing open a sleeve covering one arm of one of the bodies, and when the naked arm came in view I found tattooed upon it the same words that were tattooed upon my own arm when I was a baby:

' In this body flows the blood of Ulo !'

" I looked more closely. There was no mistake. The letters were the old letters of the written language of the Ulo and the words were the same my mother had traced in ink in my own skin.

" The writing on the arm held me chained with a weird fascination. These mummies, then, were members of the lost tribe of Ulo, members of the same tribe to which my ancestors had belonged so many centuries ago. The words of the prophecy came back to me, ringing in my ears as though spoken by a living voice. ' The Ulos are a chosen people, and a prophet shall always dwell with them to keep them faithful.' I wondered what they had thought when their prophecy had failed and they had come to die

like reptiles in an underground cavern. I wondered if the tribe of my ancestors had all died
in this gruesome cave, and if the dead bodies
before me were all that I should ever find. That
could not be, though, for the bodies before me
were all the bodies of men. I thought I might
find the bodies of the women in some other
cave—might find them, if I did not die too soon.
I tore the sleeve off the arm of another of the
bodies. There was the same writing as on the
first. Then I sat down on a rock in that dim cave
—sat down as a man from whom all fear had
gone, and I mused for hours upon the Ulos, upon
myself, upon the chances of fortune, upon life,
and death. What, then, is a man? A weak
thing speeding swiftly from a mysterious past
to a future even more mysterious; a thing of a
few days; a thing that reels under the weight
of many troubles, a thing that dies and decays
and returns to the dust of the earth, and is
soon utterly forgotten in all places in the world.
The Ulos were once a great people; they ruled
tribes whose numbers were multitudes; they
were so great that every Ulo was called a chief;
and then they went as fugitives to the caves of
the mountains,—went as fugitives and perished,

even unto the last man. They were a forgotten
race; their places were filled with other races,
and in time they also would be forgotten. Such
were the thoughts that came to me in the
cavern of the dead.

"I sat there for hours, and then, almost exhausted from hunger, I wearily climbed down
the stone ladder and began again my hopeless
wanderings up and down the winding stone
passages. Just as I was ready to give up in
despair and lie down and die, a smell of salt
water came to my nostrils, a breath of sea
breeze blew into my face, and then a few steps
brought me out again to the little bay where
my boat was moored. I ate of the food I had
in my boat, and then lay down on the rocks
and slept for many hours.

"When I escaped from the caverns I thanked
God for my deliverance and vowed that no
wealth upon the earth could tempt me to again
risk my life in the mazy passages. But when I
awoke from my long sleep and was refreshed
from my hunger and fatigue, the mystery of the
place took hold upon me again, and I set about
devising a way to safely explore the caverns,
and learn, if I could, something of the secrets

that were hidden in them. In my boat was a a great coil of common fish line that I had hastily thrown in while making my hurried preparations to escape from the ship. I unwound this line and found that there was almost two miles of it. I bound one end of the line securely to a rock, and taking the coil in my hands, again entered the underground passage, allowing the line to unwind as I walked. In this way I went on until I came to the end of the line, and I had found nothing. I retraced my steps almost back to the mouth of the cave and then set out in a different passage from the one I had been in.

"Just as I was coming to the end of the line again, I found that the passage was becoming light. It was merely a glimmer at first, then there came a soft light that showed the walls of the caverns, and then a full, steady light that one might read by. Soon the passage widened, and then I came to a large cave that was high and light, and that was fitted up as a human habitation. A large couch, made of skins and cotton cloths, lay against one side of the cave, a stone table and seat were in the centre, and various instruments, the uses of

which I did not know, were scattered about.
I discovered that the light came from the burning of natural gas that was blazing behind
shields made of isin-glass. The farther end of
this cavern was closed with a stone wall that
showed that it had been made by human hands,
and a stone door was in this wall. Upon the
walls of the room I was in were carvings,
and upon looking closely I found some words
written, or carved, in the language of the Ulos.
I blessed my mother for teaching me that forgotten language, for now it might chance that
it would save my life.

"Weary from my long wandering in the
passages, I sat down upon the couch to rest.
While sitting there, the stone door in the wall
swung open, and slowly walking toward me
came a figure exactly like one of the petrified
mummies I had found in the burial cavern. I
thought it was a ghost, but I was not frightened, so used was I becoming to terrible things.
The figure approached me, the head bent down
as though in thought, and I noticed that the
step was slow and halting like that of an old
man. Presently the man looked up, and I saw
upon his face one of the strange white masks I

had seen upon the mummies. The mask enveloped the entire head, the part covering the back of the head being smooth, and the part covering the face fitting every feature perfectly. The effect of the mask was ghastly. There were all the features, the eyes, the mouth, the nose; but all were of that same dead-white color.

"Presently the masked man saw me and stopped. He did not seem frightened, as I thought he would be, but stood and regarded me intently. Then he walked in front of me, made a low bow, and said:

"'My son, from whence came you,—from the sun?'

"I answered that I came from Mexico, and he said that he knew not that the land of endless life was called Mexico. Then I tried to tell him something of the wonderful country of my birth, but for some reason I was slow in making him understand, and I soon saw that he regarded me as a god that had been sent to him from the land of the sun.

"'What came you here to do?' he asked.

"'I came to seek the tribe of the Ulo,' I replied.

"'I am the king of the Ulo,' replied the

masked man; 'the king and the highest priest of that nation. For many years have I ruled over them, given them laws, instructed them in truth, and have offered up their prayers to the most high gods. For many years have I dwelt alone in this cavern; alone, except for the sacred snake of my people. While other men of my tribe have taken wives and have reared children, I have dwelt in this solitude, praying, meditating, and thinking thoughts of wisdom for my people. But the time of my death draws nigh; I feel my blood turn cold within my veins, and it will not be long until I must take my place among the vanished kings in the cavern of the dead. Do you know of the cavern of the dead, my son?'

"I replied that I did, and the king seemed pleased that I knew of it. Then the king brought me food, and a kind of wine made from some plant, and bade me eat and rest before talking further.

"When I had rested and refreshed myself, I talked long with the masked king, who did not seem surprised that I spoke the language of the Ulo. I learned from him that the caverns and underground passages opened on one side into

the sea, and on the other side into a valley that
was surrounded with high stone cliffs. In these
cliffs the people of the Ulo had cut their homes;
there they lived; and in the valley they grew
maize, and melons, and cotton, and various
things to eat. Beyond this valley, which was
called the Valley of Cultivation, opened another,
called the Valley of the Beasts, and in this
valley were deer and other animals hunted for
food and skins by the Ulo. The king told me
that there were six hundred people in the tribe.
He told me, also, the secret of the kingship. The
people of the Ulo believed that their king was
an immortal, and that it was death to look
upon his face. This belief had its rise in the fact
that the first king who ruled them in the hidden
valleys devised the white masks which made
one face look like all other faces. He had told
his people that he was an immortal, and would
live forever; and when his time came to die he
sent for a religious youth from among the
people, telling the people the youth was to be
sacrificed to the sun; but he told the youth he
was chosen to rule the people. Then he made a
white mask for this youth, and the people knew
not the difference, for the youth was masked

and dressed exactly like the first king, and besides, the king went but little among his people. The youth grew old; his death grew near; he chose another youth to succeed him; made him a white mask, and again the people knew not that a new king was ruling them, but thought that another sacrifice had been made to the sun. In this wise, innumerable kings had ruled over the people of the Ulo; yet the people thought it was one immortal who had always been their king. And the masked dead bodies in the cavern of death were the bodies of the men who had been kings of the Ulo.

"'My son,' said the old king to me, 'the time has almost come for me to lay down my burden of years, and take my place among the silent bodies of the kings who have gone before me. The people of the Ulo think that but one king has ever ruled over them, and it is well that they think that; but you who are to be the king must know the truth. When I was a youth I was devout in the practice of the worship of the gods of my tribe, so devout that the king often spoke to me in commendation. Now the Ulo, when they dwelt in Anahuac, gave human lives in sacrifice, giving the

lives of people they had captured in the wars.
But in this valley our numbers grew so few,
and there were no barbarians to war against,
that it was only in long periods that a human
life could be spared, even in sacrifice to the gods.
In times that were long apart, sometimes fifty
years, sometimes seventy, a youth was chosen
from among the people and sent to the king's
palace to be sacrificed. After being sent there
the youth was never heard of again, and the
king ruled apparently as before—the one called
for sacrifice being really the king. In my youth
the masked king came to me and told me I was
chosen to be offered as a sacrifice. I did not
fear, for the sacrificed ones have high places in
the land of endless life. Feasts were given,
many prayers were said, and then I went to the
palace of the king,—this same palace where I
now hold speech with you. The king instructed
me much in the wisdom of our nation, and then
he threw off the white mask and showed me he
was a man. He told me that his time to die
had come; he told me the secret of the kingship,
and appointed me to be king when he was
dead. He made a white mask to cover my face,
he taught me how to embalm the dead, (which

is done with a mineral liquid that is found in one of these caverns), he showed me the cavern where I should take him when his life was gone, and then he sent me among the people to see if I could pass as king. I went forth among the people, and they fell down and worshipped me and called me king. For I was of the size of the old king, and my voice was like his. Then the old king showed me the place where the sacred snake is kept, and then he lay himself down and died, and I was the masked king of the people of the Ulo. That was seventy years in the past, and the people know not that I have not lived forever. Now my time has come to die, and I have been meditating upon which youth I shall call to be king after me. But instead of having to choose a man to be king, a man has been sent to me from the sun. I have been a holy man and a wise prophet to my people, and in reward for my wisdom you have been sent to me, that after me you may become the sacred king of Ulo. Hail, sacred king of the land of Ulo!'

"I found that the old king was honest in the belief that he was a divine instrument, and as I am a true Catholic, I wanted sorely to try to

win him to the true faith. But he was an old
man, the hand of death was falling upon him,
and I resolved to let him die in the happiness
of his own faith.

" For many days the old king instructed me
in the mysteries and rites of the Ulo worship, for
the Ulo ruler was as much priest as king. He
instructed me in the history of his people, he
taught me the art of embalming, he told me
how to choose my successor when my days
were done, and he told me of the blood mark
that should go upon the arm of every Ulo. He
then examined my own arm, and when he found
the mark upon it he had no further doubt that
I had been sent to him as a miracle. Then he
placed a mask upon me and took me to see the
sacred snake, telling me that only masked men
should stand in the snake's presence.

" The snake was kept in a great cavern, one
half of which was a large pool of salt water
that had evidently been carried in jars from the
sea, and the other half of which was floored
with solid rock. The snake was an immense
thing, as spotted as a leopard, its length thirty
feet, and its body was as thick as the body of
a man. It seemed to be a sea snake, and I

noticed that it stayed much of the time in the pool of sea water. Horny substances, denoting extreme age, were about the snake's eyes, and it seemed to move about but very little, although I have seen it when it was as agile as any snake could be. The old king called the snake, and it went to him and wound itself around his body. The sight sent chills over me, but the snake seemed to love the man, and did not hurt him. The old king took me to the snake's cavern many times, and in time the snake would come to me when called the same as it would to the old king. But I always feared that snake, and would fear it if I should see it now, although it once saved my life. The king instructed me in the snake worship, but I need not tell you of that, as my tale is long enough without speaking of all the strange things I learned in the land of Ulo.

"When I had learned all that the old king had to tell, he bade me don a robe like his and go forth, masked, among the people, in order that I might learn as much of them as I could before he died. He gave me many directions, and it was almost impossible that I should let the people learn the secret, or discover that I was not the king who had ruled over them so long. I passed through the stone door in the wall of the cavern, passed through a number of smaller caverns, and then I went down a stone stairway into the valley. I had not seen the light of the sun for many long days, and my blood ran fast as I saw the blue arch of the beautiful sky once more. The valley seemed to have been hidden from the world by nature. It was about one mile wide and about six miles long, and at the farther end was a narrow pass or cañon that opened into the Valley of the Beasts, a place where I never went. As I went down the steps I saw the homes of the Ulos that had been cut out of the solid rock of the cliffs. I saw men and women working in the fields, and as I drew near them, walking slowly as the king had told me to do, they ceased from their labors and raised their arms in salute to me.

"'See, the king comes,' said one man, 'the king, who has come down into the valley but once since the feast of the harvest of maize.'

"'It may be that he comes to choose a youth to be sacrificed,' answered an old man. 'It is seventy years since a sacrifice has been given, and I doubt not the gods hunger.'

"My voice was much like that of the old king, and I had schooled myself in imitating him, but my knees trembled when I first spoke to the people.

"'My children,' said I, 'I have not come to choose a sacrifice; the gods of our people are well content; our people are wise and worshipful, and it may please our gods that no human life will ever again be offered as a sacrifice.'

"The people did not answer, but they gazed at me curiously, and I thought I saw a scowl upon the face of the old man who had spoken. He was a barbarian in his worship, and the thought of human sacrifice was dear to his heart.

"I walked entirely through the valley of Ulo, drinking in every new scene, but seeming to notice nothing. When I was returning to the palace in the caverns I met a party of young girls going home from the fields where they had been at work.

"The girls were young, ranging in age from twelve to sixteen years, but they would have seemed much older to any one who lived in a land where women do not develop so rapidly as in that warm clime. They had soft, black eyes and raven black hair, and were dressed in kirtles and skirts made of cotton cloth. Upon their heads they bore pottery jars filled with water from a spring in the mountain side.

"My attention was immediately attracted to one of the girls on account of her wonderful beauty. Her features were as finely chiseled as the features of the most patrician queen, her form had the perfect proportions of a statue, her black eyes were as soft as the eyes of a dove, and her wealth of raven-black hair fell in silken masses to her knees. She was not brown, as many Indians are, but red, as are many of the women of the Pueblo tribes. As soon as I saw her my heart went out to her in love, and I determined to win her if such a thing might be. I did not stop to consider that the laws forbade the masked king to look in love upon any woman, nor to think of the danger and trouble I might bring upon the maid and myself if I sought to win her. The maidens tripped merrily along, and I heard the beautiful one called by the name Lo-Zeenah. That name in the Ulo speech means Beautiful Star. The maidens saw me, bowed in worship, and I passed on my way to the caverns.

"That same day the old king died. I bathed him in the petrifying fluid and placed him in the Cave of Death. Then I was alone in the cavern palace. Alone, with no living thing to bear me company, no book to read, no work to do.

"The next day after I had walked in the valley there came to the outer rooms of my palace a deputation of the old men of the tribe, asking that I sit in judgment upon a charge preferred by the war-chief against the maid Lo-Zeenah. The Ulos had not been in war for centuries but they held the tribal formation of the olden time, and the war chief was one of the great men of the nation. The present war-chief had craved Lo-Zeenah in marriage; her father and mother had given consent, but Lo-Zeenah herself had persistently refused. The refusal was a breach of law. Lo-Zeenah could be punished, even unto the taking of her life, and in anger the war-chief had brought a trial before the king. If the chief had known that under the austere robes of that masked king there beat a young heart on fire with love for the beautiful Lo-Zeenah, I think he would not have begun the trial.

"I consented to sit in judgment upon the cause of the chief and the maid, and they, and nearly all the people of the tribe, came before me, just outside the hall of my palace. The angry chief came with a dark brow, intent upon revenge for the slight put upon him; the people came with sorrow written on their faces, for they all loved the Beautiful Star; and the maiden herself came with a gentle presence that won all hearts to her. But the laws of the Ulo were deemed inexorable, and all expected that the king would decree that she should wed the chief or lose her life for disobedience. I knew there was danger for even the king to go contrary to the laws, but I would have died before inflicting either punishment upon the beautiful girl that stood before me. The case was stated to me while I sat like a carven statue upon my stone throne of judgment. When all had spoken, I said:

"'People of Ulo, the laws of our nation were named by the fathers of long ago. They are just laws, and they cannot be evaded or revoked. You all know that in this case the maid should wed our war-chief, or that her life should be taken in punishment. Even I, your

undying king, could not change this law, unless
Those Above should bid me. I am not sure of
their will, though, for in a dream it has lately
been revealed to me that the people of Ulo
shall again become a great people, of whom
every man shall be called chief; they shall
again become the rulers over many peoples.
In that dream it was shown to me that a
woman of the Ulo shall be chosen by Those
Above to be the mother of another king, a king
who shall take part of the tribe and go forth
in strange places to extend the sway of the
nation. Those Above have promised to send
me an image of this woman who shall be
chosen to become the mother of a king, and
until that image comes I shall pass no judgment upon any woman in the land of Ulo.
Therefore this cause shall be held in abeyance,
waiting the pleasure of Those Above, whose
chosen people the Ulos are. Those Above have
said that the image shall be wafted down from
the mouth of the entrance to my palace, and
shall fall in the valley. Go, then; set men to
watch in the valley for the image, and when it
has fallen, will I decide. Until then Lo-Zeenah
will abide in the inner rooms of my palace.'

"The people were greatly excited when I had thus spoken, and all the old men and the chiefs murmured because I had decreed that the maid should remain in my palace. It was against the sacred laws for any woman to be alone with the king; and an old priest, the father of Lo-Zeenah, rose in his place and said his daughter should not go. He said he was a true son of Ulo, a wise, a just, and a holy man, in whose eyes rebellion against the king was a wicked thing; but he loved the laws and the wisdom of the fathers even more than he loved his king, and he said he would lose his life in battle with me before the sanctity of the religion should be profaned.

"Much excitement was caused by the speech of the old priest, and the people began taking sides, some with me, some with the old man. The war-chief, who desired to wed Lo-Zeenah, was a fierce man with a dark face, and he rose in his place and openly accused me, the king, of being guilty of sin in desiring to have a woman in my palace. I was afraid a rebellion would take place, but I made no sign of fear. I rose in my place, stretched out my hand, commanded silence, and said:

"'Oh, thou fools! thou fools, who dare question the wisdom of your holy king! Know you not that I can stretch forth my hand and cause you all to die?'

"The women and some of the men cowered in their seats, but the war-chief and the old priest laughed and said that although I was a king they knew I could not kill. Again I rose in my seat. 'Go forth,' said I, 'and bring to me a fawn. And while the hunters are gone for the fawn let no man speak nor leave his seat.'

"I knew I was in danger but I felt so sure of success that I could have sung a song while waiting for the hunters to bring the fawn. The hunters soon returned with the fawn, and I commanded them to leave it at a certain spot about a hundred paces from me. Then rising in my seat I pointed my revolver at it and said: 'Die!,' fired, and the fawn rolled over dead.

"It was a simple thing, of course, to you and me who have known fire-arms all our lives, but to those simple Indians who had been immured for centuries in a lost mountain valley it was nothing else than a miracle, and the people covered their faces in fear of me, who could bring death by stretching forth my hand. They saw the fire leap from the revolver's mouth, and they believed that I could have killed them all with a wave of my hand. I noticed that, while the war-chief trembled like the others, his face was yet black with hatred, and I commanded him to stand before me. Slowly he took his place before my stone throne, and I said:

"'You, oh war-chief, have harbored hatred of your king in your heart. It would be just if I should kill you as I have killed the fawn, but I am a merciful king, and your punishment shall be tempered with mercy. Instead of killing you, I will place upon you an everlasting mark that shall warn others never to harbor hatred for the king. From now to the end of your life you shall carry the mark of the avenging fire of my wrath, and if ever again you shall show hatred for me, the fire that now enters your hand shall enter your heart and you shall die and be accursed! Hold up your right hand!'

"The chief held up his hand, and all the time his face was ashen with the fear of the supernatural punishment. I took aim with the revolver, fired, and the bullet sped through his

hand, leaving a hole in the palm. The people hid their faces in fear. Never before had their king shown his wrath in such a terrible way. But when they began to fear me they began to hate me and I had sown the seeds for the ending of the reign of the masked king of Ulo. Again I spoke to the people, and said:

"'Now, oh people of Ulo, return to your homes and your fields. Hunt in the Valley of the Beasts, say your prayers to the sun, but never again say one word in opposition to your sacred king. And remember that I have willed that Lo-Zeenah the maid remains with me.'

"The people rose when I had concluded, and, bowing low before me, left my presence in fear and trembling. Lo-Zeenah remained behind, gazing at me with her star-bright eyes. When the people were all gone she came before me.

"'Oh, King,' said she, 'you are merciful. The people reviled you and you did not kill them. You are merciful and just, and I, your daughter, revere you more than ever.'

"I took the maid with me, went through the stone door to my private palace, and talked much with her, not telling her that I was not

really the Ulo king. She was a beautiful crea-
ture as she stood before me and it was hard
for me not to tell her of my love for her. Her
mantle only half concealed the fair proportions
of the wearer; her hair was loosed and fell in
flowing profusion to her knees; and she was
the most beautiful woman I had ever seen. I
found her to be a maid of wondrous purity
of mind. All her life had been passed in the
narrow valley of Ulo, but she was as wise as
many people who have roamed to the ends of
the earth. I asked her why she had not loved
the war-chief, and she answered that he was
a man who was no better than the brutes that
roamed in the Valley of Beasts.

"With my photographic camera I made a
picture of the girl and showed it to her.

"'Oh, King,' said she, 'and am I then the
one chosen to be the mother of a king? I,
Lo-Zeenah, a simple maid of my people! Do
you think that I may be good enough and pure
enough so that this great thing can be? And
may I go forth with the new tribe—go forth
over the cliffs and the mountains, and see the
breadth of the beautiful land that was made
by the great gods of Shi-pa-pu? Oh, King,

often have I sat in the valley and watched the
birds fly over the cliffs, and I have longed to
be free like them, to roam at will over the
beautiful earth. For the earth must be beautiful, as it was made by the gods. Never has my
heart turned in love to a man, as have the
hearts of the other maids of our people, and
sometimes I have feared that my longing for
beauty and for a wider life might keep me from
loving any man of Ulo, and I might go childless
and loveless down to my grave.'

"Such was the speech of Lo-Zeenah. Do
you wonder that I loved her more as I knew
her more?

"At sundown I took the picture I had made
and walked to the precipice that was at the
end of my palace. Looking down into the
valley through a hole in the rock, I saw old
men sitting in waiting for the image I had
promised them. Standing back so they could
not see me I threw the picture, and I looked
through the hole in the stones to see it fall.
The old men saw it as soon as it fell, and
picking it up, gazed upon it in wonder. Then
they raised their voices and cried out:

"'Oh, people of Ulo, the words of the great

prophecy have been fulfilled. The sacred image has come from the gods, and Lo-Zeenah, the Beautiful Star of our nation, is chosen to be the mother of the unborn king! Oh, people of Ulo, Lo-Zeenah is the chosen one!'

"Then the people took up the cry, and as the sun went down I could hear them chanting, 'Lo-Zeenah is chosen! Lo-Zeenah the beautiful is the chosen one of Those Above!' And then I went back to my palace in the caverns to talk with Lo-Zeenah.

"I was but a youth then, Señor. The hot blood of my young years was coursing in my veins, and it was hard for me not to clasp that fair girl in my arms and tell her all the tale of my love for her. But I feared the result, and I treated her as an old man might treat a little child. In time she and I came to know each other well. I told her that the religion of the Ulo was about to change—told her, by degrees, of the one true faith, and in time we came to know each other so well that I told her the blessed story of the Great Redeemer of the world, and I baptized her as a follower of the Nazarene. Then I removed the white mask from my face and stood before her as my true self. She gazed upon me first in fear, then in wonder, and then the soft light of love came into her beautiful eyes. I told her the true tale of how I came there. I told her all the story of my life. I showed her the hall where the dead kings lay. I explained to her the mystery of the revolver and of the picture, and then I said:

"'Lo-Zeenah, sweet one, now you know me as I am. I am no god and no king. I am but a wayfaring youth whom fortune has sent to the strange land of your people. I came here seeking adventure; I found you and love, and now my future, my very life, is in your hands, for a word from you will cause your people to fall upon me and take my life. But I love you, Lo-Zeenah, more than ever maid was loved.'

"She smiled, her soft arms went round my neck, her sweet lips pressed mine, and I knew that Lo-Zeenah loved me. The memory of that time abides with me to this day as the sweetest and best time that was ever in my life, and it will abide with me and cheer me even unto the time when I shall cross the dark valley of death.

"How we lived from then on I need not tell you. But to me the pearly vales of heaven could not have been a more blissful abode than were those stone caverns by the sea, where my loved one dwelt with me. We were young then, Señor. We had never loved before. Does not that tell you all? And as men may do in barbarian lands, I took her as my wife, intending to have the sacrament performed when we were where a priest could be found. Such marriages are recognized by our church.

"Lo-Zeenah listened in wonder to the tales I told her of the places in the world that lay outside of the lost valley where her life had been lived. She was glad when I told her I would take her to those places, and she entered into plans with me to convert the people of Ulo to Christianity, and then to go to Mexico together to live. In time I told the people something of the new creed, and, while they greatly feared me and my mysterious power, they were so angered that they stoned me. I tried for many days to teach them, but their anger grew worse. In time they tried to kill me, and I was compelled to retreat to the inner palace and barricade the passage.

"Then the Ulos, who had a hatred for everyone, even their king, who tried to profane the old religion, sought to come upon us by climbing into the caverns. The war-chief succeeded in reaching the passage that led from the palace to the sea. He found my fish-line and tore it up, and then he entered the palace. His leering face had no sooner come inside the palace than a bullet entered his brain, and he fell dead before us. Then were we prisoners; a savage race on one side, a maze of winding passages on the other. But in spite of our danger we were happy, so great is the power of love to lighten the dark places of life.

"One day we were planning of the life we would lead in far-away Mexico, and wondering if we should succeed in finding our way to the sea, when we heard a muffled beating at one of the inner doors of the palace. I had heard the same sound in the old king's lifetime, and knew it was made by the snake, but I feared to admit it, as Lo-Zeenah might be afraid. I told her what it was, and she said:

"'My loved one, is not the snake one of God's creatures, the same as you and I? I would not fear anything that God has made.

The snake may not be so beautiful as the birds, or the fawns, or the flowers, but it came from the wisdom of the great father of wisdom, and we should love it, and not fear it.'

"I opened the stone door and admitted the snake. I was masked and it did not know me from the old king who was dead. It wound its slimy folds about me and reared its grisly head high in the air. Then it saw Lo-Zeenah, the first unmasked person it had seen for long years, and a hiss came from its mouth. It quickly unwound itself from me, reared its horny head high in the air, and before either of us comprehended what it might do, it struck Lo-Zeenah a mighty blow full in the face,—struck her, and bit as it struck—and she fell back, dying from its poison! I clasped her in my arms; I besought her to live for my sake; I wept tears of the most bitter grief over her; but she was doomed, and I could not save her. She drew my head down to her soft bosom; she pressed sweet kisses to my lips, and then she died in my arms, with a sweeter smile on her face than I ever saw on the face of any woman. All the time the ghastly snake reared its ugly head high in the air, coiling and uncoiling the

" It reared its horny head high in the air."

UNIV. OF
CALIFORNIA

slimy folds of its body, and sending forth shrill
hisses that made my blood run cold. All the
world had grown dark to me; the caverns of
Ulo seemed to me like the caverns of Purga-
tory; all the brightness had gone from my life,
and I prayed that merciful death might come to
me there by the side of my dead loved one.

"When my grief had somewhat spent itself,
I arose and struck the snake on the head with
my hand. I hoped that I might anger it so
that it would bite me, but it cowered and slunk
in fear. In some older time a masked man had
conquered that terrible reptile, and it still feared
the power of the mask. I trampled it, and
struck it with rocks, but the more I beat it the
more it cowered in fear. Then I took my revolver and tried to kill it, but the bullets fell harmless against its thick hide.

"I took the body of Lo-Zeenah and em-
balmed it and placed it in the chamber of the
dead kings. There it lies to this day, the most
beautiful thing that is hidden from the sight of
the world. Then I strove to make my escape,
and I greatly missed the guidance of the line.
I wandered for hours in the caverns and passages, and at last, worn out with weariness

and despair, I found my way back to the palace, that place where I had known so much joy, and where I had known grief that was blacker than the gloom of the grave. The snake was still in the palace lying prone on the stone floor, its tongue hanging out as though from thirst. Its craving for salt water would have sent it back to its own cave, but the stone door through which it should have gone was closed. My grief was so great that I paid but little heed to the snake; and worn out at last, I lay down and slept for hours. When I awoke I saw the snake still lying where it had been.

"I feared that I would never find my way out of the caverns, and that I was doomed to die there alone under the earth. Some of the people of the Ulo knew the windings of the passages, but I dared not go to them. As I was pondering on my hard fate I saw the snake raise its head and move it from side to side, as though seeking something. A thought struck me, and I believed that the snake might be made to lead me to the sea. I had a jar full of salt water that I had used for bathing, and I took it and held it before the snake's head. The snake seemed almost dead, but the smell of salt water animated it; it reared its head high and emitted a sound that was almost like a groan. Again I held the salt water to its head, and then, as I moved away, it followed me until I set the water down. By carrying the water, I led the snake to the mouth of the passage that led to the sea, and then I threw the water as far down the passage-way as I could.

"Old memories that had lain dormant for years seemed to be revived in the snake. It reared its head until it struck the top of the cavern, and gave vent to almost human groans; then it dropped its head to the earth, raised its tail, as a snake does when it runs, and with a shrill cry started off down the passage. I believed that some old king, long years before, had captured that snake from the sea and brought it through that passage-way, and I believed that it would find its way back. I grasped its horny tail in my hands as it crawled, and I followed it through the dark passages, that were dripping with water that had soaked through from the mountain tops.

"Slowly the snake crawled along. It paid no heed to me, although I clung to its tail,

and it constantly gave vent to moans and cries
that were almost human. Sometimes it stopped
as though puzzled, and then it went on again,
winding its way through the mazy tunnels.
Once it stopped and remained still a long time,
and I almost despaired, for I thought I should
be lost and should die—I and that ghastly
thing, hidden deep in the bowels of the
mountains.   Then the snake went on again,
slowly at first, then faster, then haltingly
again, until we turned a sharp corner of
the passage, and a faint smell of the sea came
to my nostrils. . The snake smelled it, too; it
reared its head, a loud cry came from it, and
then with the speed of a race-horse it sped
down the passage-way.   It had smelled the
sea, the scent of its native element had come
to it, and its age and weakness seemed to fade
away as a mist fades before the sun.   It sped
onward so rapidly that I was almost thrown
from my feet, but I clung to it, and as we ran,·
the smell of the sea water became plainer and
plainer.   Soon the passage became light, the
wind from outside blew in my face, and then
with the speed of the wind the snake drew me
forth from the caverns, and I stood once more

by the side of the little bay where my boat was moored. There again was the beautiful sky that I had seen but once in months; there was the blue water of the bay, sparkling in the sunlight, and beyond the stone walls of the cliffs I could hear the surf beating upon the rocks. It would have been a glad time to me if it had not been for the sad memories of the beautiful one I had loved and won and lost in the hideous caverns of Ulo.

"When we came to the salt water the snake was like a thing demented. It twisted its huge body in hideous coils, it wound and then unwound itself, it reared itself upward until it seemed to stand on its tail, and then with a shrill cry it leaped off the bank and threw itself into the water. It shrieked as it struck the water, it dived and rose again, it laved its body, and then, with a long, shrill, almost human cry, it raised its head, as a snake does when it swims, and it sped away through the rocky pass to the broad ocean, and I saw it no more.

"I remember that hideous snake almost as though it were human. It both loved and feared the old Ulo king, and it feared and loved me because I seemed like him. It was a prisoner, and for how long it had been a prisoner no man can tell. It had been stolen from the ocean, had been imprisoned in the rock caves of Ulo, and it seemed to me that it had held a hatred for all things but the priest, hated them because it was a captive. It had killed Lo-Zeenah, but it would not kill me, who courted death from it, and it had saved my life by leading me down the mazy passages to the sea. If it had not been for that snake I might now have Lo-Zeenah for my wife; and if it had not been for it, too, my bones might now be rotting in the caves of Ulo. It was one of God's creatures, and it must have been created for some good use. *Quien sabe?*

"That is about all my tale, Señor. I found my boat as I had left it, unmoored it, steered it through the rocky pass, and set sail in the open ocean. Within a day I was sighted by a small sailing vessel that ran between the Isthmus and San Francisco. The ship took me on board; its men jeered at the tale I told them, called me crazy, and the ship landed me in San Francisco. I returned to Mexico, and after a time I went again striving

to find the rockbound bay that leads to the
valley of Ulo. I searched the entire west coast
of Mexico from Guaymas to Acapulco, but I
could not find it; and I do not believe that any
man after me will ever find the lost tribe of Ulo.
It is well, too, for people like us not to find
them, for they are a heathen people, who hold
a hatred for everything outside of their own
lost valley, and we belong to remorseless nations that would reduce that proud tribe to a
nation of beggars and outcasts and serfs. The
Ulo are ignorant, and as intolerant as ignorant
people always are. But they are not a bad
people, else how could one so pure and good
as my lost Lo-Zeenah have been reared among
them? I suppose they found out long ago that
the masked king was gone, and I think they
may have a new king, for heathen minds can
always find something to worship."

The mellow night held the world in the
mystery of its beauty. The town of San Marcial slept on in the moonlight. The Mescaleros
lay motionless under the cottonwood trees, and
the kronking of a tree frog was the only sound.
The Mexican sat in silence for a while, his face
buried in his hands and his mind wandering

back to that time when he had known love and joy and peace as he dwelt with his nut-brown bride in a cavern by the sea; then he raised his head and said:

"Is not the night beautiful, Señor? There is much trouble, and bitterness, and sorrow, and suffering upon the earth, but God is over all, and the world is very fair if our eyes are not too blinded to see its beauties."

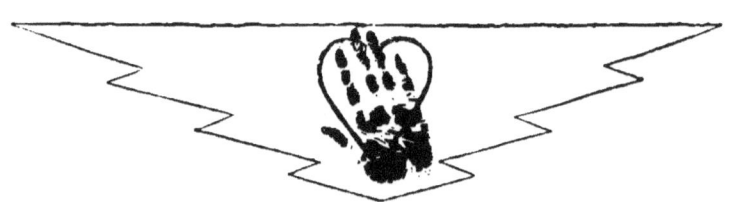

LOST PUEBLO

AM an old man, and my name is Hak-ki. I am a son of Lost Pueblo, and in my time I have seen stranger things than were ever seen by my fathers or the fathers of my fathers; and as you are a white-skinned wanderer who tells me strange tales of your great land in the North, I will tell you the true tale of Lost Pueblo, a place that is now deserted and unknown to men, and the tale of my nation that, save me, is vanished from the face of the earth.

In the old time of the long ago there flourished a prosperous pueblo in a fertile valley among the blue mountains of the land that the white-skinned men now know by the name of New Mexico. The people of that pueblo had been known as wise people for generations unnumbered; its fields were rich, its houses were many and large, and its *shamans* said that the *Shiuana* looked upon it with great love, and that the pueblo and its people were very dear to the Great Father who dwells in the sun. The men of the pueblo were brave warriors who had won many scalps from the savage tribes who dwelt in the wild country surrounding their fields, and the *shamans* said that the sons of that pueblo would never be conquered. But a witch must have been born among that people, for in an evil hour their glory began to fade and their prosperity to diminish. First the rains came not in the months of rain, and the crop of maize was blighted, and the people hungered and were nigh unto starvation; then the savage Apaches who dwelt in the wild country came down upon them in hordes, killed the flower of their young men, carried the women away as slaves, destroyed their houses and even their sacred *estufas*, and the old men of the tribe sorrowed because the anger of the *Shiuana* had fallen so heavily upon them, and they knew not the cause. Sacred dances were held; the *shamans* fasted until the life was almost gone from their bodies; the men, the women, and the children stood upon the house-tops and prayed, and

" They stood on the house-tops and prayed."

sacrifices were offered; but instead of smiles from the *Shiuana* there came a strange and unknown disease, and many people were mowed down by death and hurried on the road to the Land Above.

In that old pueblo there was a young man of great bravery who sorrowed much that his people were so sorely stricken, and although he was not a shaman, he went into a cave alone and fasted seven days and seven nights; and then it was revealed unto him that the pueblo of his fathers was grown too populous, that the people were too many to live from the lands, and that the wars with the Apaches and the ravages of the plague were but visitations sent to reduce the number of the people, to destroy some so that all might not die or be forced to engage in unholy war with each other for food.

This warrior told of what had been revealed unto him in the cave, and many of the wise old men shook their heads and said he lied; but many young men and young women believed in him, and asked of him what he thought might be done that they and their fathers might not die nor engage in unholy

war each with his brethren, which would be
worse than to die. The young warrior knew
not what reply to make, and to gain wisdom
he went again to the cave and fasted for three
days and three nights more, when it was revealed unto him that he must select one person
from every six who dwelt in the pueblo, and
with them go to a strange land and found a
new pueblo that should be a home for him and
his friends and the children of him and his
friends. And when he spoke of this to the
young people of the pueblo they believed that
he spoke in true words and not in lies.

So it came about that a great dance was
held, and then the warrior and one man out of
every six men, and one woman out of every six
women, and one urchin out of every six urchins
in the pueblo took bags of maize and meat and
seeds, and put them on their heads or slung
them on their shoulders, and they all set out
toward the land where the sun is when the day
is three-fourths dead. For six days these people
journeyed, and the sun was hot and the way
was weary; and on the morning of the seventh
day they came to a high mountain that rose to
the snow, and around which there seemed to be

no pass. The warrior sent men to seek for a way around the mountain, but in one day's time they returned with sad faces to say that there was no way.

Then the weary men were sorry in their hearts, and the women fell on their faces and tore their hair; but the warrior was of good cheer, for he knew that he had been guided aright. The warrior bade his people eat and drink and gain strength, and after three days of resting he bade them climb the mountain. The men grew angry and called him a fool and the son of a witch; but he told them that to return to their fathers was to starve, that there was no pass around the mountain, and that if they believed the *Shiuana* did not lie they must believe that their way led across the top of the mountain. Then the men who had murmured were ashamed. and they all began to climb the mountain. The way was of rocks and hurt their feet, and as they went higher it grew bitterly cold, and the people were almost ready to lie down on the wild mountain and die; but the young warrior, whose name was Looki, cheered them, and told them that they must surely find a beautiful land ere many days. And just as the strongest men were giving up in despair, Looki gained the crest of the mountain of snow and sent up such a shout of joy that his voice reached even the fainting ones who had lain down and refused to go farther. The people were cheered by Looki's voice, and they gathered their strength and struggled to the crest of the mountain, where it was very cold because of the snow, and where there were no trees. But when they reached the very top, and could look down on the other side, their hearts were very glad, for far, far down below them there was a beautiful green valley, all shut in by high snow mountains, in which there was green grass and many green trees, and herds of deer and of bison.

On the sides of the mountain nearest to the valley there were springs from which the water flowed forever, and the people rejoiced and knew that that valley was their Promised Land. But the side of the mountain nearest to the valley was so steep that even a wild goat of the mountains could not go down, and the people knew not how to descend. Again the young warrior sent away a man to search for a way to get into the valley, and, although it was very cold on the top of the mountain, the people did not complain. The man returned with a sad face and said that there was no way; but again Looki was of good cheer, and he told the men to take their garments and the women to take their robes and to tie them all together one to the other; and when this was done they fastened the rope of clothes to a crag of rock, and one by one the people took hold of the rope and perilously climbed down from the mountain of snow into the beautiful valley of grass. When the last one was down they pulled at the rope of clothes until it broke from the crag, and they all had their garments again. Then they turned their faces to the Father in the Sun and gave thanks that they had been safely led to a new home in a far country.

When they were all safe in the valley they killed bison with arrows and had food, and then the women began to build houses, and the men planted the seeds they had carried from the pueblo of their fathers. And that was how there came to be founded the pueblo that in all the old pueblos was forever after known as Lost Pueblo.

In the old pueblo there were no tidings heard

of the people who had gone forth, until after two harvests had gone by, and the people believed their children had been slain by the wild Apaches while making their journey. But one man who had gone forth with the wanderers returned to the pueblo of his fathers, and he was half crazed, like a deer that had eaten of the poison loco, or like a man that had been bewitched by some vile bird. When he was fed and had rested he told of the journeyings of the wanderers, and of the new pueblo they had builded in the green valley. He had tired of the new pueblo and had longed for the land of his fathers, so he had climbed the high mountain of snow and come home. He was so near to starving and to dying from cold that the strength of his mind had gone from him, and when he tried to lead the men to the new pueblo he could not, although he tried for many weary days; and the men who dwelt in the old pueblo never again heard of their children who had gone forth, and forever after they spoke of them as their children who dwelt in Lost Pueblo.

The people who builded the new pueblo in the valley longed to hear from their fathers again, and they tried to find a way over the vast mountains of snow that shut them in on every side, but they could find no way, and they too named their home Lost Pueblo. And for six hundred years these people and their children and the children of their children's children lived out their lives in Lost Pueblo, which was in a green valley six miles one way and two miles another way, and was like a pit cut in the face of the mountains. They worshipped the gods of their fathers, they kept green the memories of all the knowledge that was known in the old pueblo, and after six hundred years had gone into the past the people of Lost Pueblo were a wise people, being even as wise as their forefathers who had found the valley. It was in my lifetime that the nation of the valley was six hundred years old, and among that people I was a chief and a priest.

When I was a young man there was born into my nation a male child who was named Say-Len; and when I was becoming an old man Say-Len was a strong young man, and such another young man had never lived in Lost Pueblo. He was so strong that he could do the work of two strong men and find the work to be but play; he was so gentle that he would leave the council to soothe a crying child; and he was so brave that he longed to be a warrior and make war for his people; and when the fathers told old tales of the wars our forefathers of the old land had fought six hundred years before, the heart of Say-Len was heavy within him, for the people of our Lost Pueblo knew no other nations, and there were no savage tribes to make war upon. Say-Len looked upon the walls of our valley as a captive looks upon the walls of his prison, and he longed to cross those walls and learn if the sons of our people still dwelt in the old land among the mountains. Say-Len loved a maid of Lost Pueblo, and for her sake, and to show her how brave he was, he longed to scale the mountains, to go forth to the old land of his forefathers, and to learn what manner of men and of things were in the world that lay beyond our narrow valley. The old men of the nation were sad because of the longings of Say-Len, and his mother and the maid he loved also besought him to remain among his own people and be content. He paid no heed to their entreaties and he daily tried to scale the mighty walls of living rock that hedged in the valley of our home. It sounds like a lie to say it, but it is true that in time he climbed out of the valley. He himself could never say how it came about that he was able to climb out, but he believed, and I believe, that he had the help of the Shiuana, who are good to brave men. When he had climbed out of the valley, then were the hearts of our people very heavy with sadness, for Say-Len was the bravest son of our nation, and we never hoped to look upon his face again.

As the years passed away we prayed to our Great Father in the sun that he would guard Say-Len wherever he might wander, and that if he lived he would bring him back to his own people. But the time was so long that we did not think our prayers would be answered. For five years the people of Lost Pueblo heard no word of Say-Len, and all but the maid he loved believed him dead; but the maid refused to wed with any other, saying always that she believed Say-Len would return to her. The maid believed a truth, for in five years the wanderer returned to his own land and his own people.

One day I was tilling maize in my field, when I heard a great shout go up from the pueblo, and I hurried to my house and found the people gazing up at the great snow mountain that rose above the valley; and on the top of the snow mountain there stood a man who waved a white cloth to the people. The fathers and priests of our tribe were afraid and counselled together, and they thought the strange man must be a witch or an evil spirit, and they brought arrows to shoot him; but in all my life there had never been such a glad time to me, for I knew it was Say-Len who stood above us, and when I told my people, their cries of fear were turned to such shouts of joy as were never before heard in Lost Pueblo.

Say-Len had a great rope with him, and he fastened it to the same crag on the mountain that the people had fastened the rope of clothes to in the old time; and when he had come down on his rope he left it tied to the crag, so that any one who would might use it to get out. I am the only one who ever climbed that rope, and it was so hard to climb, and so long was the way, that I was almost content to let loose and fall and die in the valley.

" And the death wail was heard afresh in every hour. "

Say-Len came home at an evil time, and he found his people in great trouble. A rift had broken in the side of the high mountain where the springs were, and water was running into the valley faster than there was any way for it to get out. Already the lower maize fields were destroyed; in two moons it would surround the houses, and the oldest and wisest of all our people could not tell where this water came from.

When Say-Len had come down the mountain and was again among his own people, we saw that he bore the looks of a man who had borne a great grief. He greeted us, and then ran to the house of his own clan and caressed his mother, and then he sought out the maid that was dear to him, and caressed her, and then he told the old men to call the people together and he would speak to them. I am an old man and a chief and I have seen many years go into the past, but the speech of Say-Len was the strangest speech that I have ever heard.

Say-Len told that his heart had failed him when he had reached the top of the snow mountain, and that he longed to return again to the valley, but could find no way. He rested on the top of the mountain, and then began to climb down on the other side, going down in the same way the people had climbed up six hundred years before. As he climbed down the mountain at first he came only to naked rocks and snow, but soon he came to small trees and then to flowers, as it was the time of spring, and then he was off the mountain and was in a great valley of sand that stretched away farther than the sight of his eyes could carry. He could see so much that he was afraid at first, but soon the sun came from behind a cloud and then he was not afraid; for the sun shone into the valley where he had lived his life; the sun was the home of the Father of his nation, and he knew it was good for him when the sun smiled upon him. He then set out across the wide valley of sand to seek the old pueblo whence the forefathers of his forefathers journeyed six hundred years before. He journeyed six days and slept six nights, and on the seventh day he came to two long pieces of iron that stretched across all of the valley; and he knew not what they were for. He sat down by the pieces of iron to think, and men with white faces who were dressed in strange garments came over the iron, being

drawn by a mighty thing that breathed out
smoke and fire. Say-Len was not afraid, for
the people who wear the head-bands and side
locks know not fear, and the men stopped their
mighty thing and took Say-Len with them.
They gave him strange food to eat and strange
things to drink, but when he asked them of the
pueblo he was seeking they shook their heads
and did not understand. Say-Len did not understand the speech of the white-faced men, but
they took him with them away to the North
and away to the East, much farther than he
thought the world ran. They took him to the
great pueblos of their own people, and Say-Len
has told me that such wonderful pueblos are
known to no other nations except the blest
ones who dwell in the bright pueblos of
Shipapu. The white men taught Say-Len the
language of their people, but he did not teach
them his language nor tell them of the valley
where his nation dwelt, so they knew not of
what nation Say-Len was, and they called him
a Pueblo Indian.

For five years Say-Len dwelt among the
white-skinned people, and he told us many
tales of the strange things he saw among them.

He said the white-skinned people dwelt in a great land that stretched from the sunrise to the sunset, that their pueblos were of greater number than the numbers of the stars in the sky. He said that the people had wires that talked, wires that gave forth a greater light than is given by the sun, machines that draw loads, machines that do the work of men, and that they had more gold than the valley of Lost Pueblo would hold. But he said they were an unwise people and an unholy people, and he loved them not. They love gold so much that they seek it through all their lives, and will not even take time to stand on their house-tops to pray. They have great riches, yet the poor people in the great pueblos die for the want of maize. The gods have blessed them in all ways, but they love not the gods and forget them in their seeking after gold. Say-Len said the simple life of his own people was nearer to the heart of God than was the life of the white nations; and he tore the strange clothes from his back, donned again the garb of his own people, took the maid who was dear to him for wife, and took up again with gladness the quiet life of his own people.

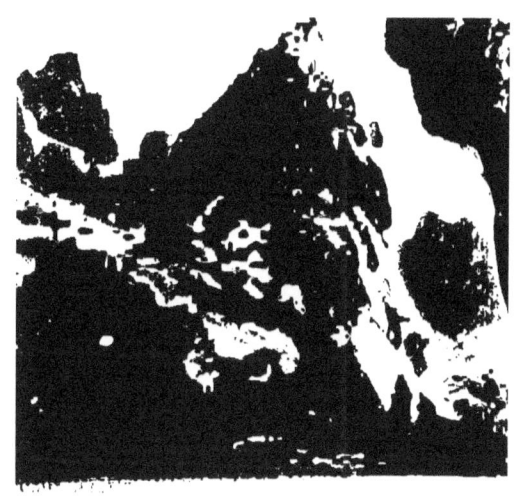

"The mighty waters that cover Lost Pueblo."

Evil seemed to pursue Say-Len, the bravest son of Lost Pueblo, and the second day after he took his wife, even while the marriage dance was being celebrated, he was stricken down with a hideous plague, called by him the small-pox of the white-faced people; and in three days more he died, and his spirit joined the spirits of his fathers above. While he was yet being prayed across the bad land that lies between life and Shipapu, others were stricken with the plague, and soon it came about that the death wail was heard afresh in every hour. Death dwelt in our valley from that time on, and during the rising of forty moons the people of Lost Pueblo had all died, and my nation had faded from the face of the earth—all but me, who am an old man whose memories are full of sorrow, and who would be better dead.

I know not why I escaped the plague unless it is that I am a wise *shaman* who fasted much and who am loved by those above. I stayed in the deserted valley of my birth and kept the sacred fire burning and prayed for the souls of my people, until the waters from the rift had reached the houses; and then I climbed the rope that Say-Len had left hanging from the crag,

and I came to the valley of sand and wandered
to the iron road and across it until I came to
this pueblo, which is a pueblo of the people of
my own blood and whose forefathers were one
with my forefathers more than six hundred
years ago.   Here I am welcome although a
stranger, and here will I dwell until my burden
of years falls from me, and I can join my people
in the fair land of Shipapu,—that bright land in
the sun, where Po-so-Yemmo sits at the right
hand of Yo-See, and where peace, and plenty,
and joy, and freedom from sorrow and death,
will be known throughout the countless years
of an endless forever.

"I am an old man, and my name is Hak-ki;
my nation is gone from the face of the earth,
the ancient home of my people is covered with
the cruel waters, and there is no more joy for
me in living.   I am an alien in this pueblo, and
it cheers me to talk with you, who are a white-
faced man of the same nation that was known
to Say-Len, and I tell you this tale because you
have seen strange things, for you tell that the
mighty waters that cover Lost Pueblo have
also made a great water called the Salton Sea.
I know not how you know of this, but I believe

you speak in true words, for the great knowledge and the strange tales of your nation pass
my understanding. I believe the strange tales
you tell me; but I believe your own great people
know no stranger tales than the one I have told
you of my lost nation and of the Lost Pueblo
where I was born.

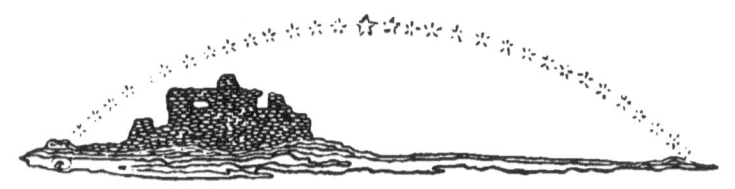

ETRA'S name was Sayla. That is, her name had been Sayla until the missionaries had come to baptize all the children in the pueblo, and they then gave her the name of Petra. The missionaries were so anxious to win the Indians from all their heathenish ways that they did not even allow them to retain their old names. Of all the children they baptized, there were none more comely than little Sayla. Her parents were among the poorest people in the pueblo, yet they always managed to keep her well dressed. When the times were too hard with her father for him to trade for blankets with the Navajos, her mother wove blankets out of wool that she earned by working for the medicine chief. Sayla, or Petra, was so bright and pretty, and learned so rapidly, that two mission teachers, who came

to the pueblo, determined to send her to school in an Eastern city. Petra cried a great deal upon leaving her mother, for her father had died just before; and many of the oldest and wisest men in the pueblo shook their heads and said it would be better if Petra stayed in her own pueblo and married a man of her own people.

They thought it was better for a woman to learn to grate corn and to plaster houses than to learn to read and write, and the other useless things the white people learned out of books. But Petra was ambitious, and she went away to school.

One day I was wandering about the dusty, crooked little streets of an Indian pueblo. As guide and interpreter I had a fifteen-year-old Pueblo boy, who had been educated at Santa Fé, and who spoke Spanish and English as fluently as he spoke the dialect of his own people.

I had met two other men who could speak a very little English, and had found one girl who could say, (thanks to the efforts of a mission priest), that the house of her uncle was greater than the house of the brother of her aunt. That was all the English I had expected to hear in that isolated village in foreign America, and I was, therefore, somewhat surprised upon entering an unprepossessing little mud-hut to be accosted with:—

"Good morning, sir."

The woman who thus addressed me smiled in a ghastly manner. She was one of those peculiar-looking people whose age is difficult to determine. One of her eyes was out, her face was rather wrinkled, there was a perceptible stoop in her shoulders, and her thinness was in marked contrast to the plumpness common to the Pueblo women. The usual placid contentment of the Pueblo women was also lacking. She was barefooted, clad in a single garment, and in her arms she held a little girl-baby, who was nearer naked than herself.

My interpreter went out to watch a game of *patol* that was being carried on in the shadow of a mud wall, and I sat down on a long seat, covered with blankets, that ran along one entire side of the room, lighted my pipe, and made ready to listen to the tale of Petra.

"No, *amigo mia*, I am not proud that I speak English; instead, I am sorry. There was a time when I was very proud that I could talk in the language of the great *Americanos*, and there was another time when I hated every word in the language, and every white-skinned man and woman who spoke it; but the troubles that gave me the fierceness have also taken the fierceness away, and now I am only sorry. I am glad to see you and to speak to you in your language. I speak it so rarely that I almost forget it, for here we speak only Teguan and Spanish. The sight of you takes me back to a time when I was a happy girl. Are you not hungry? Will you not eat?

"Yes, I will tell you my story. I am,—in your language it is called a Magdalen,—and I am now hated by all the people of this pueblo— hated so much that when my little girl grows up she will not be allowed to play with the other children.

"My father was a poor man, and my mother, who still lives, has always been a poor woman. I have no brothers or sisters. When I was a little girl a Spanish priest came here from Mexico to baptize the little children and to learn if the people were yet loyal to the holy faith. He liked me, for I was pretty and bright when I was a little girl, and he taught me to speak Spanish. That *padre* went to Mexico and died, and then a priest came to us from Baltimore, and with him came two women who kept a school to teach the Indian children. The Indians did not send their children to school, and the women went away, and when they went they took me with them. I was then of the age of fourteen, and was old enough to be married to Pablo Bateis, who sent his mother to ask for me; but I wondered about the land of the white people, and I would not marry him, preferring to go away with the women. It was a good school where I lived, and there I learned English and many other things. I translated the poem of 'The Raven' into Spanish, and my teacher sent it to Madrid, where it was published in a newspaper. That was considered a great thing for an Indian girl to do.

"When I had been three years in the school I greatly liked the ways of the white people, and would have lived among them always, but they told me I must go to my

own pueblo, and teach the Indian women
to live as the white women do. I was very
glad to be home again and glad to see my
mother; but I grew tired of the pueblo in a
little while, as the people did not want to
learn new things, and it seemed very dull to
live just the same life over and over again
one day after the other. The people did not
like me very well either, for I wore the dress of
a white woman, and the wise old men of the
tribe did not like that I should be different
from the women of our own nation. Those
wise old men are fools who do not know as
much as the wild coyotes of the plains, and
there was a time when I hated them enough
to kill them. They will smile and seem pleased
when the missionaries teach their children, and
then they will take the children to their own
homes and tell them that the missionaries are
fools, and that the wisdom of the white men
is not so great as the wisdom that has come
down to the Pueblo peoples from the Fathers.

"I could not go back to the school again,
and I did not know how to earn my living
among the white people. At school they had
tried to teach me not to live as an Indian, but

they had not taught me how to live in any other way. So, although it was dull here, I put away my fine dresses, donned the costume of my own people again, and began anew the life of an Indian woman. This pleased the people of the pueblo, and for a time they treated me better. Can you not give me some whiskey? I want it only for medicine—only for medicine, I assure you; and I feel very sick.

"One time there came a white man to live in this pueblo. He was an ethnologist, and he came to study the lives of the Pueblo Indians. The governor liked him, and took him to live in his own house, and the man studied our language and made pictures of us. When this man saw me I spoke to him in English, and he was greatly surprised that I could speak it so well. He came to see me every day, and talked to me about books, and about the great cities he had seen, and he asked me many questions about my people. One day I showed him a little picture I had painted, and he stroked my hair and said I was a civilized heathen. It was not long until this white man told me that he loved me; and I loved him more than I loved any other thing on the

earth.   He was very different from the slow
men of my nation, and he said such nice things
to me.   In time he came to our house to live.
He said we would live that way until time for
him to go to his own home, and then he would
take me with him to his home, and marry me.
My own people were angry with me, as they
think a Pueblo woman should not wed any but
a Pueblo man.   I cared little what they thought,
for I was happier than any other woman in
the world.   I could have gone away with that
man and lived with him forever alone in a
cave in the mountains.

"One day I came home from the fields
where I had been to gather green maize, and I
found this man asleep on some blankets on the
floor.   I stooped down and kissed him, very
gently, so as not to waken him.   He often
slept in the daytime, and when he slept I was
always very quiet so as not to disturb him.
This time he had fallen asleep while he had
been reading a letter, and he held the letter and
a small picture in his hand.   An Indian had
been to a Mexican town where there is a post-
office, and he had brought the letter.   I went
out in the shade of the wall to prepare the

maize, but I could not work for thinking of the letter he held in his hand as he slept, so I entered the house again, lay down by his side very gently, and I read the letter and looked at the picture.

"Do you know how it would seem if the one dearest to you on earth should all at once become the thing you hated most?

"That was the way I felt, for the letter was from his wife, and the picture was a picture of his wife. That man was a white devil, and he had lied to me and told me he had no wife. I knew then why he always delayed marrying me, and I knew he was a liar with a black heart. I knew that when he tired of me he would go his way and leave me to be reviled by my own people. He lay there sleeping, with a smile on his face; but he was nearer his death than he had ever been since he was born.

"I ought to have killed him; I think it would have been better if I had killed him and then killed myself; but I only maimed him. My father had an old stone ax that had come down through many generations. It was an ax that had been used long ago in the wars

with the Navajos, and its edge was as sharp
as the steel axes of the white people. I took
the ax and with one stroke I cut off the
hand of the sleeping man—the hand that held
the letter. Then I stood over him with the
ax in my hand and cursed him; and he was
a coward, and he cried like a baby. Then I
ran away from the house and away from the
pueblo, and I hid in a dry *arroyo* for twelve
days, with nothing to eat but yucca roots
and wild berries. When I came back the man
had gone, and the people of the pueblo looked
at me with hatred. I stood on my housetop
and cursed the people, and to this day I hate
them and they hate me.

"If you will give me some more whiskey,
I swear to you that I will drink but a swallow.
I am really sick, and the whiskey gives me
strength.

"Well, that is about all. When my white
lover was gone, no Indian would marry me,
and I became what I now am. I could not go
to another pueblo, as the Pueblo people do
not like outcasts. I could not go among the
white people, for, in spite of my education, I
was nothing but an Indian. The people all

UNIV.
CALIFOR

"I stood on my housetop and cursed the people."

hated me, but in the silence of the night the men would steal into my house, and they would bring me the whiskey they bought in the Mexican towns. Not all the men of course; only those who are almost as wicked as the white men. One time when I was drunk I cut a man with a knife and he tore out my eye with his hand. When the people were putting herbs on my eye I thought of the time when I had translated the poem of 'The Raven.'

"My life now is a bad life. When I have whiskey I am drunk, and when I am not drunk I am worse, for then I hate every white man in the world, and every Indian, too. Will you not give me more whiskey? Please let me keep it all. Whiskey is all I live for, and I am very poor, so poor that it will be a long time before I have money enough to buy any for myself.

"To talk with you reminds me of my life in the schools. Ah, they teach wonderful things in the schools! Have you read the poems of Homer? I love to read them. See? I have two books of the poems of Homer, and I read them every day. These fools around me cannot read. They tell old tales of the Fathers, and make prayers to the sun, and they think they are better than I. I am twenty-one years old, and it is four years since I came from the schools. Ah, curse those schools and the people who teach in them! But for them I would not be able to read Homer, but I would now be a happy woman. Is there not a poem in your language about the bliss of ignorance?

"Good bye. I trust I have not wearied you with my doleful tale. If—if you can give me a little money I will always pray for you, for I am a poor woman and I need money very badly."

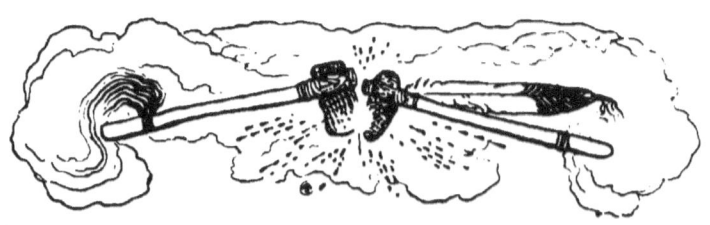

THE BRUJA BONITA

 LUMBERING in the placid sunshine of the Rio Grande valley lies the little mud-built pueblo of Santa Clara, one of the historic Indian villages discovered by Coronado, and whose people and their ancestors, according to their own traditions and the conjectures of the archæologists, have dwelt in beautiful Santa Clara cañon and the cliff houses of Pu-Yé for more than sixteen hundred years. To one who sees the place for an hour or a day, and does not see into the lives of its people, it seems like a dream-village hidden away from the turmoil of the world, whose inhabitants seem to have eaten of the lotus and to care for naught but rest and peace.

But of all Indian pueblos, Santa Clara is the most turbulent, and its inhabitants the most quarrelsome and vindictive. A feud rages in the

village, and grows more bitter as time goes on.
At first it began over the right of a particular
man to succeed to the great office of *cacique*,
that peculiar office whose incumbent is at once
ruler, priest, wizard and prophet. It was al-
leged that the succession to the office, in the
case in point, was irregular, and that the man
who claimed, and secured the office, was an
impostor.

Matters went from bad to worse; two
factions sprung up, and one evil day the
governor of the pueblo soundly pummeled the
sacred face and form of the *cacique*. The
latter's adherents proclaimed that the great
spirits would cause most dire punishment to be
inflicted upon the wicked governor. But no
harm befell him, and his faction gained new
strength from the ranks of the enemy. Finally
the feud grew until neutrality was no longer
possible, and every householder was enrolled in
the ranks of one of the opposing factions.
Members of the opposing factions often fought
with hands or clubs, and sometimes knives
were used, and guns threatened. Revenge was
sought in every way by both sides, and consisted of every sort of retaliation, from destroy-

ing crops to acrimonious accusations. One member of the faction of the governor estranged the affections of the wife of a man of the opposition, and the case was brought before the council of the *principales*. The wrong-doer was fined a burro and a goat, which he paid to the injured husband, and then he lay in wait for him behind the wall of the *estufa*, and the two men fought in the dust of the plaza, to the edification of the small boys and naked girls who played together regardless of the squabbles of their elders.

The feud still continues, and seems to grow worse with the passing of the years. The government officials who investigate the condition of the Indians gravely predict that there is serious danger of an outbreak in the pueblo, in which many members of the warring factions will be killed. And Santa Clara is a place from which those who yearn to see the Peublos dwelling in picturesque peace had better keep away.

The buxom widow of Po-tseh became involved in the feud, and when sitting by her mud fire-place molding little images of the rain-god, or husking blue corn in the sunshine in front of her door, many were the acrimonious things she said about the governor and his faction. The widow's husband had been a strong adherent of the governor, but luckily for his chances for domestic felicity, he died when the vendetta was still young. After his death the devoted widow cut her hair in mourning, and wailed the death-wail, as a sorrowing widow should. But while she was mourning, she kept a "weather eye" out for such good-looking young men as had found no help-meets, and it was hinted that she even looked with secret favor upon staid heads of families and fathers of children. The widow grieved for a full month; then one day she went to Española, bought a quart of very bad whiskey, and in the morning was found drunk in her house in company with an Indian whose reputation was far from good.

Widowed Mrs. Po-tseh, it thus appears, was a woman of congenial and convivial tastes. She was of so hospitable a nature that many a warfaring Indian from a neighboring pueblo, or Mexican who chanced to be journeying up or down the valley, was entertained in her house through the long nights of winter or the lonesome nights of the summer time, when the village was quiet, and the working people all asleep. And in the second year of her widowhood she became the mother of twin babies, two brown little girls, who were half Mexican and half Pueblo. The children grew up with the Santa Clara feud, and until they went to Santa Fé to school, they knew not that all peoples did not waste the sweetness of existence in factional hatreds.

The two little half-breed babies were baptized in the big adobe church that frowns so gloomily upon the Rio Grande, and one of them was given the name of Carmelita, and one was christened Alicia. They had other names as well, old Indian clan names that they never heard except among their own people. Carmelita's Indian name was "The Beautiful Duck with Pink Feathers Under Its Wing," but as that was rather an elongated cognomen, even for an Indian, the brown little maid came to be known only by her "church name" of Carmelita. Alicia also had a long Tewan name, but as it grew into disuse early in her career, and as it would make quite a draft upon space, it will be omitted here.

Carmelita, in appearance, favored her Mexican father, while Alicia was of the Indian type, and resembled her mother in every way. When a mission school was opened in the pueblo, Carmelita attended daily, and soon learned to speak well in the Spanish language. Alicia loved best to throw mud at the mission teacher and then scamper across the bare plaza, and her mastery of the soft Castilian speech was very slow. Then the two girls went for a year to the school at Santa Fé, and when they returned, they were two plump young maids with rounded forms, and the eyes of swains of both factions to the feud were cast in admiration upon them. Alicia soon forgot her year among the teachers, became a partisan of the *cacique's*, and in many ways gave evidence that she was the daughter of her mother. Carmelita sided with the governor, but on feast days was always partial to the Mexican visitors, and was not well liked by the clannish people of her race. In time she fell in love with a Mexican herder, and took no pains to conceal her preference, and then the people of the pueblo were more unkind to her than ever.

When Carmelita was fifteen years old, she had developed into a woman, as do the daughters of the Rio Grande valley, who become women in form while they are yet girls in years; and the brother of the ruling *cacique* sought to win her for his wife. She detested the man, who was a brute and a drunkard, and flatly refused to marry him. Contrary to the usual Indian custom, her mother attempted to coerce her, but to no avail; and, in the heat of anger, she drove Carmelita from her house. The girl found shelter with one of her relatives, a deaf old widow who paid but little heed to the comings or goings of the girl; and for many days her mother and sister refused to speak to her. Carmelita cried a great deal, but she remembered that Faustino Lucero loved her, and she believed that as soon as he should come to the pueblo to again visit her, all would be well. And it might be, too, that Faustino, seeing she had no home, would marry her and settle down with her to live happily in one of the vacant houses of the pueblo. The people might object a little at first, but such things had been, and might be again, especially as the governor liked her. Faustino was a Mexican, it was true; but was she not half Mexican herself? And the lines of blood and clan had come to be almost forgotten in the degenerate days of the feud and the encroachment of the Mexican and white settlers in the valley.

While Carmelita was longing for a visit from Faustino, a member of the *cacique's* faction died in his bed of blankets one night, and was found cold and stark in the morning. No perceptible ailment had afflicted him, and a hushed whisper went among his sorrowing kindred to the effect that a *bruja*, or witch, might be in the pueblo. The next day the little daughter of the deceased man was found dead in a small field, where she had gone alone to gather corn. And then a toothless old crone remembered that the dead man had one day spoken crossly to Carmelita, and that she had made a sharp answer to him. The next day a snake bit the sacred ankle of the *cacique*, and while his brother was bandaging the wound, he suggested that Carmelita hated the *cacique* and all his people. The snake bite was not serious, and was not from a venomous reptile; but the mere fact of having been bitten at all, and of hearing the whispered allusion to Carmelita, caused the worthy *cacique* to retire to the fastness of his secret chamber, and meditate for four days. While he was fasting, the members of the medicine order looked askance at Carmelita when they chanced to meet her, and she began to feel that some great danger threatened her.

And then Faustino came. He reached the pueblo on the afternoon of an October day that had been set aside by the Indians as a day of rest. He rode a brown pony, and he wore a wide hat with a silver band about it, and a beautiful red necktie was tied like a knotted rope about his neck. In his pocket was a pouch of tobacco for the *cacique*, a pint of whiskey for the governor, and a little mirror, a bag of candy, and a photograph of himself, for Carmelita. He rode through the upper plaza with a clatter, and galloped down into the lower plaza, where Carmelita dwelt. Before he dismounted from his pony he saw in the door of an upper house a face that was to him the most beautiful face in the world, and he threw his reins over the pony's head and climbed the rude ladder before he had had time to speak to any of the few Indians who were loitering about. The two retired into the room, a pair of plump red arms went around the Mexican boy's neck, he was greeted with a kiss, and the dark locks of Carmelita were hanging over his shoulder, where she had pillowed her head.

"Carmelita *mia!* How is it with you the long, long time since I have seen you? I cannot say to you how lonely has been my heart since I last was here, and every day I have longed for my *bonita* sweetheart who dwells in Santa Clara. But a great *gringo* from Colorado has been in the valley buying sheep, and he paid me twenty *pesos* a month to help drive his flocks. I went as far to the north as Antonito, and I say to you, *dulce,* that never have I seen such a city as is that one of Antonito. The windows of the houses are like great looking-glasses, and the *tiendas,* oh, loved one, how can I describe to you those wonderful *tiendas!* All the goods that are known in the world are there for sale, and in some of them as many as four men are selling beautiful things at once. It was there that I got this for the most beautiful girl that lives in all the world," and he drew from his pocket the little mirror.

The girl's breath came short and fast as she gazed upon the trinket with greedy pleasure, and then again her arms went around the brown neck of the boy.

"But how is it with you, *amante?* And why are you here instead of at your mother's house? Come, let us go there," said Faustino.

Then Carmelita explained the sad happening to him, and also told him of the looks of suspicion that were cast upon her since the deaths and disasters had occurred in the pueblo.

"And I fear, sweet Faustino, that the wicked brother-in-law of the *cacique,* whom I refused to wed, will try to make the people believe I am a *bruja.*"

"A *bruja!*" laughed Faustino, kissing her. "Well, you certainly are the most *bonita bruja* that ever breathed the air or changed men into animals. But," his face darkening, "this must not be. It is a very, very evil thing to be a *bruja,* and the luck is very bad when one is called *bruja* falsely. If these people come to think you are a *bruja,* they will kill you."

The girl's eyes fell, and the boy's eyes filled
with tears, for he had lived in the Pueblo country all his life, and knew that the Indians were
even more relentless than the ignorant ones of
his own people in the hunting out and killing
of witches.   But danger yet seemed afar off,
and with the true Mexican spirit he preferred
not to go halfway to meet trouble, so he
threw off his cares, and again began to chatter
joyously to his sweetheart.   Her spirits rose
with his, and soon they had almost forgotten
that such a thing as danger was in the world.
The old aunt of Carmelita, with whom she
lived, came in, saw Faustino, greeted him
warmly, counselled Carmelita to get him food,
and then withdrew as should a wise aunt who
has no need for an extra niece to be a per-
manent incumbrance upon her house and larder.

Then there was an hour that will always be
remembered by Faustino and by Carmelita as
well.   They were only a Mexican youth and a
half-breed Indian maiden, seated on an adobe
settee in a second-story house in dull old Santa
Clara; but the theme they had to talk about
changed all their surroundings for them, and
they were as happy as though the little mud

pueblo had been a marble city, the second-story house a palace, and they a king and a queen. For love was with them, and it drove care from them and made them forget all sorrow and all time but the happy now. What they said need not all be written here. Though the words were simple, the language was sweeter to them than any other they will ever hear.

Faustino invoked any number of Spanish saints to bear witness to his great love for Carmelita, and while she knew already that he loved her, it made her very happy to have him tell her so, over and over again.

"And, Carmelita," said the boy, "Am I not a grown man now? See! my mustachios are so long that they can be seen at a distance, and my mother says I will not now grow any taller. You are full-grown, too; and if the good saints will send just one more *gringo* to Española for sheep, and I can be employed by him for two months, then can we be married. I have saved twenty *pesos* from the last *gringo's* employment, and in two months more, I could save forty more, and then we would be very rich, for, besides all the money I should have, my mother says she will give me a burro and a cow, and the field that lies next to our house, when I am married. Will we not then be very rich?"

"But does your mother say you may marry me?" asked the girl, suspiciously. "I fear she will not consent that you marry an Indian, and if she does not, cannot we be married anyhow and dwell here in Santa Clara?"

"Santa Clara is very beautiful," said the boy; "and with you I should be very happy here. But the people here hate each other so much, and some of them would hate me; and we should be far happier in the new house I shall build close to my mother's house on the north."

"The people here would not hate you; they could not, for you are so good. And I fear your mother will not consent that you marry me. Does she not still desire that you marry the daughter of your neighbor, Señor Baca?"

"Yes, she does so," replied Faustino, his countenance falling. "But I have so long worked for my mother that she loves me very much; and when I at last go to her and say I will never be happy any more in the world until I have you for my wife, then she will

kiss me, and say to me that I may bring you
to her. Then will you kiss my mother and
say you are her daughter, and then the *padre*
will marry us, and we will be happier than
people ever were before."

"May the saints speed that happy day,"
said the girl. "But go now, and put your
pony in the corral, and when you return I
will have the supper ready, and you and I
will eat it here all alone, just as we shall
do when we are married."

Faustino climbed down the ladder, singing
a song about a happy squirrel that lived in
a piñon tree, and after he had put away
his pony he went to deliver his presents.

The *cacique* did not rise from where he
was sitting before the fire, nor did he speak,
but he took the proffered bag of tobacco.
His taciturnity made an impression upon the
Mexican, for, taken with his sweetheart's fear,
he felt it boded no good. The governor took
the pint of whiskey with muttered thanks,
drank some of it, and buried his face in his
hands to again plot vengeance upon his hated
rival. Much depressed, Faustino went again
into the plaza and there met Alicia, the sister

of Carmelita. He spoke to her, and she replied shortly. Then she asked why he was at
Santa Clara so late in the day.

"Why, to visit with your sister, the *bonita*
Carmelita; for what else?" said Faustino,
gayly. "You are very pretty, Alicia, but all
the great beauty of your mother, and your
grandmother, and your grandmother's grand-
mothers for two hundred years, was saved up
by the saints and given to the *bonita* Carmelita at her birth."

"*Bonita*, yes; but a *bonita bruja*," said
Alicia, gruffly, as she turned and shuffled away .
in the twilight.

Faustino again climbed the ladder that led
to the home of Carmelita's aunt, and found his
sweetheart alone in the room, busily engaged
in preparing a supper. She was sitting on the
cement floor of the room, before the odd little
fire-place, and was cooking *tortillas*, while a
squirrel was simmering over the fire. The ruddy
blaze of the piñon fire shining into her face
made Faustino think he had never seen her so
beautiful before, and after gazing upon her for
a moment from the doorway, he put his arms
about her neck and kissed her.

"Sweetheart, *mio*," he said, "to see you busy with the cooking like a little house-wife, makes me long all the more for the time when we shall be in our own little *casa*, and can sing to each other and caress each other, and tell tales to each other from morning to night. Will that not be a glad time? We will have some goats, and a burro, and it may be that in time I can make enough money by working for the rich *gringos* to buy another pony, and then we can have a wagon and drive to Española on Saturdays, and to church at Santa Cruz on Sundays, like a real Don and his Señora. And on the day of the great *fiesta* of Santa Clara, we shall come here and see the dance, and on every such day you shall have a new gown."

The girl had been listening with pleased and wide-open eyes, but her countenance saddened when he mentioned the *fiesta*. She said :

"No, Faustino, we will not come again to Santa Clara when once we are away and have a *casa* of our own. The people here are my people, with them I have always lived, but they like me not. My mother passes me by without a word, my sister frowns upon me, and even now I doubt not that the *cacique* and the medicine men are talking as to whether they should kill me for a witch. It is a sad thing not to have the love of one's own people; yet I think your people are more my people than are these folk of Santa Clara, for I am more Mexican than Indian. I like not the ways of this place of my birth; I like not the *cachina* dance, that knows not modesty; I like not this worship of times that are long gone from the earth, nor the hatred for knowing new things that the people of this place hold. Glad will be the day when we are gone, and when I can let my hair grow as a Mexican woman, and dress as do the women of your people. But come, our food is ready."

They ate for a time in silence, and just as they had finished, an old Indian came into the room. He sat down taciturnly, and gazed into the fire for a time in silence. He did not live in that house, Carmelita was no relation to him, and the young people wondered why he was there; but they said nothing. Soon the old man turned from gazing into the fire, and said:

" He gazed into the fire for a time in silence.

" Friend, is not the pony you rode here to-day a swift runner. "

" Yes," answered Faustino.

" Do you sleep all the hours of the night?" again asked the Indian.

" When I am herding the flocks, or driving cattle for the *gringos*, I am glad when comes the hours of sleep. But when I come to Santa Clara, where I have many friends, I care not much to sleep," replied the boy, half smiling.

" Times come when it is good not to sleep, and when it is doubly good if one have a fast horse that will not rebel if two people ride him at once," said the old Indian. And giving the young Mexican a meaning look, the Indian drew his blanket about him, and went out of the back door of the room, climbing down on the side of the house that faced away from the plaza.

When he was gone the two lovers gazed at each other with wide-open, questioning eyes. Why had the Indian spoken so strangely? Was there danger for them, and was he trying to give them a guarded warning to mount Faustino's horse and leave the pueblo? But if the medicine men intended harm to Carmelita, it would be

impossible for them to leave without detection.
And with troubled faces the two lovers sat, with
clasped hands, and gazed into the dying fire.
Faustino well knew the horrible punishment
inflicted upon *brujas*, and his mind was filled
with terrible visions of his Carmelita, hanging
by the neck to the wall of the *estufa*, while the
crazed men shot arrows into her quivering
flesh.   He thought of the horror of seeing her
body, denied a proper burial, burning slowly to
ashes, as the red fanatics danced about it, and
reviled it, and shot arrows into it.   And in
misery he clasped the Indian girl in his arms
and wept. The situation was too sad to permit
of much conversation, and for two hours the
lovers sat silently embracing each other, while
the darkness of night grew thicker and denser
over the little mud pueblo.

Without warning the door of the room
opened, and the two lovers sprung to their feet
with affrighted gasps.

They expected to see a band of half-naked
and painted men, coming to bear Carmelita
away to the torture; but instead, they only
saw Carmelita's sister, Alicia.

Alicia went close to the two cowering

people, lowered her voice to a whisper, and
hurriedly said: "Carmelita, you are my sister,
and when I come to speak truth to my own
heart, I know that I love you more than I
love any other person in the world. I am
a bad woman, and you are a good woman,
and because you are good and I am bad, I
have tried to make myself believe I hated you
and wished you harm. When the words went
forth among the people that it is you who
are the wicked *bruja* who causes all the
trouble here, I did not deny it, and I even
helped to spread the words and cause you
harm. I knew not what I did until to-night,
but I have just been in the plaza listening to
the making of medicine in the *estufa*. I listened
through a hole in the wall where I could hear,
and the people knew not that I was there.
They are making ready to kill you, sister;
and when the hour of midnight comes, unless
you go away before, strong men will come
here and bear you away to your death.
Faustino they will not harm, for he is not
of us; yet if they become crazed, as men do
who seek *brujas*, they may even harm him.
You must get away to a place of safety.

And it is you," turning to Faustino, "who must get her to such a place."

The three stood gazing at each other with distended eyes, too frightened to know what to do or say next. Carmelita was first to recover the use of her faculties, and she took her sister in her arms and kissed her. She said:

"I cannot get away, sister, and to try would only be to place Faustino in danger. But I have no fear. I am glad that you are to me a sister again, and that I may tell you that I love you as I have always loved you. And you, Faustino, know that I love you above all the things of the world,— love you so much that I will not have you endanger yourself for me. You can stay with me another hour and be safe; and then you must go down into the plaza, and tell those whom you meet that I am a *bruja*, and that you are leaving me as soon as you learned the truth. Then take your pony, and ride away while it is yet safe; and before they begin to torture me."

The girl fell into her lover's arms, and nothing was said. In all their simple lives not one of them had ever faced death and danger and misery and degradation all at once, and the awfulness of the situation dazed them. While they were standing silent, with terror-stricken faces and sinking hearts, a soft whistle was heard coming from the ground below the rear door. They all started in new fear, and stood like frightened antelopes awaiting the attack of wolves. Again came the soft whistle, and then the sound of a man stealthily climbing the ladder was heard. Faustino involuntarily drew himself to his full height, grasped a bowie-knife, and stood ready to defend his sweetheart as long as he could. Carmelita sunk into a heap on the floor, and Alicia, with a wicked expression on her Indian face, also drew a knife and placed herself in an attitude ready to spring upon the invader. Then the door was gently opened, a white head covered with a flaring sombrero cautiously appeared in the aperture, and the new-comer quickly glanced over the room and at the occupants. Carmelita was so frightened that she believed it was the devil incarnate, who was glaring at her with eyes which her fevered imagination magnified to four times their real size. Faustino only clutched his knife with a firmer grasp, and

awaited the time to spring and strike. But
Alicia's face cleared, she let her hand fall to her
side, and she gasped the word "Miguel," and
looked wonderfully relieved.

"Miguel," however, became suddenly animated, and with a cat-like spring he was inside
the door, had drawn a big six-shooter from his
holster, and had a "bead" square on the
middle of Faustino's forehead.

"Drop that knife, you infernal greaser, or
I'll bore a hole through your black head," said
the white-headed one, in a cold, even, but very
business-like voice.

"Peace, Miguel, all is well," said Alicia;
"and peace, Faustino, for Miguel is my friend,
and will not harm you when he knows what
we have to tell. It is thus, Miguel; the makers
of medicine believe my sister to be a *bruja*, and
we think that to-night they will strive to take
her to the torture. Faustino is her lover, and
he and I, hearing your step upon the ladder,
believed it was the war-chief and his men come
to take her away, and we were going to try to
defend her for a little time, until too many of
them came for us to stand before. But the
good spirits have sent you instead."

Faustino silently sheathed his knife, the man called Miguel put his revolver away, and Carmelita, somewhat recovered from her paroxysm of terror, rose to a sitting posture. The white man stared blankly at the others for a full minute, then said " Well I'll be damned!"

The sudden relaxation of the situation, and the change from supposed danger to momentary safety, caused the four persons to stand for a time in stupid silence. Then the white man turned with a grin to Alicia, put his big hand on her shoulder, and said:

" Look here, my Loo-loo Daisy, don't you remember that you are under contract not to call me by that greaser name Miguel any more. My name is Michael, Mike for short,— plain Michael J. Wentworth, and I don't stand being called Miguel. If you were a Mexican and a man, instead of an Indian and a girl, I'd shoot holes in your boots and make you dance, while you apologized for calling me names ;" and the big, white face of the blonde Missourian separated its upper and lower parts in what was a very large and voluminous grin.

Mike Wentworth was a cowboy, or cowman, as he preferred being called. He had an abiding hatred for Mexicans, towns, and the ways of civilization; and he had about explained the situation when he had called Alicia his "Loo-loo Daisy." Alicia, like her mother, was a woman who loved wine, song and the opposite sex; and she was not, in any wise, a stickler for any of the proprieties. Mike had met her once, when driving a herd down the valley past Santa Clara, had struck up a friendship with her, which he explained to himself by saying she was not so foolish as a white woman nor so dumb as a Mexican; and she had become what he was pleased to call his Loo-loo. As soon as Mike understood that Faustino and Alicia had not been making ready to "carve" each other, he said:

"Shucks, young feller, I almost took a shot at you just for luck, for I thought you was pulling your knife on the girl. But if those howling idiots had been after you instead of it being me just coming up here in a peaceful frame of mind to find my Loo-loo, you wouldn't have stood any more show than a rabbit. You see, me and a pardner of mine are taking the chuck-wagon of our outfit down the valley, and as our camping place is only about a mile from

here, I thought I'd come over and hunt up Alicia
and some other likely young Indian girl, and
we'd go over to the camp and have a little
jamboree. But, seeing you're all in a sort of
box, I think I'll give up the gay-Lothario racket
for the time being, and try to get you and your
girl out of the mess. Now let's get down to
the facts of the situation."

All the time he was talking Alicia had gazed
at Faustino with a half-shamed, half-wistful
expression, and a moisture that was danger-
ously near being tears came into her eyes.
Faustino, who knew something of the ways
of cowboys and Indian maidens, showed no
surprise. Carmelita looked reproachfully upon
her sister, but said nothing.

Mike scratched his head and thought.
Presently, he said :

" Young feller, you are sweet on Carmelita,
as I gather the facts ? "

"She is my sweetheart," said Faustino,
simply.

"Same as Alicia is mine," said Mike, grinning. "But what are you going to do with her?
If you let her stay here, she will be killed ; and
if you don't let her stay here, it kind o' follows

that you've got to take her away, and what in blazes will you do with her if you do get her away?"

"I will marry her," said Faustino.

"The devil you will!" said Mike, in real surprise.

"I will marry her. Why not? I love her," said the Mexican.

"Well, its catching before killing," said Mike, "and if you don't get her out of this ancient and historic hell's half-acre, your chances for a wedding are slim. Let's see; suppose you and I draw our guns, put Carmelita ahead of us, march out of the pueblo, and shoot any red-skinned galoot that tries to stop us. This ain't the right century for hanging witches. Our good Puritan forefathers, who knew all about the intentions of the Creator, had the run of the range on that cheerful pastime, and the rights ended with them. Are you willing to make a try at waltzing out and taking our chances?"

"You must not expose yourselves," said Carmelita. "The people will be frenzied if they see me escaping, and they will kill us all."

Michael J. Wentworth strode up and down the dimly-lighted little room, his head hung

low in thought, and his lips involuntarily giving
vent to profane ejaculations that were not com-
plimentary to believers in witchcraft or to
Indians in general. Finally he stopped and
carefully inspected Carmelita and Faustino
in turn.

"By gad, I believe it'll work," he said.
"They're about the same size, and one sweet
consolation is that their hides are the same
color. It really was a great scheme to invent
a Mexican out of an Indian, a Spaniard, and
more Indians! May blessings be upon the head
of old man Cortes and his inventive and amor-
ous soldiers," and the cowman deliberately
began to measure the width of Carmelita's
shoulders with his hands.

"What do you intend?" asked Faustino.
"What plan have you for escape?"

"Why, if you ain't afraid of being strung up
for a *bruja*, I'd like to have you get Carmelita's
togs on and stay here to stand off the gang,
while the girl gets into your duds, and just
politely ambles out of the pueblo with me. I
allow that your duds will fit her, and if they
do, it stands to reason that you can wear hers.
And with Mike Wentworth peacefully and po-

litely escorting a Mexican boy out of the pueblo, at a time when foreign society is not wanted, I think I can get her to my camp in good order."

The proposition met with great favor, and Mike climbed down the ladder to take a walk in the plaza, while the change of garments was effected. He met an Indian prowling along the wall, and spoke to him, and when the Indian answered, discovered that it was a man he knew.

"Why are you in the pueblo at this time, Miguel?" asked the Indian guard, suspiciously.

"Just to have a little 'go' with Alicia," answered Wentworth, carelessly. "Here is a dollar, *amigo*, with which to buy yourself some whiskey, for medical purposes only. How goes it in the pueblo?"

"The time is bad," answered the Indian, clutching the dollar. "Have you not heard of the evil times that have come? And do you not know that the maid Carmelita, the sister of Alicia, is a wicked *bruja*?"

"*Bruja*! Jumping Jerusalem! Why that's tough, ain't it?" answered Mike, in well feigned surprise. "Are you dead sure she's a *bruja*?"

"There is no doubt," answered the Indian.

"And what will be done with her?" asked Mike.

"That is for the *cacique*, the governor and the *principales* to decide," answered the Indian, stolidly.

"Well, then, I reckon I had better *ramos* from here. Don't you think so?"

"It is not well that you remain here," answered the Indian.

"And I'd better get the boy Faustino to *ramos, tambien*, do you not think?"

"Does the Mexican know the girl to be a *bruja*?" asked the Indian.

"Oh, no, he don't dream of such a thing. He's just a simple boy and knows nothing. I will tell him, and get him to go away with me. It is very, very bad to be a *bruja*, and I am sorry I have talked with one," said Wentworth, with a rueful expression.

"It is well that you and the boy Faustino depart," said the Indian.

"All right, *amigo*," answered Mike. "And as you are the only Indian I know that can talk United States, suppose you go ahead of us a few feet to explain, if we happen to meet

any of the muck-a-mucks that have charge of
doing up the witches."

"It is well," answered the Indian. "But
few of our people can talk in the language of
the *Americanos,* and I will go ahead of you to
tell the people who it is that leaves the pueblo
in the night."

Wentworth climbed the ladder again, muttering as he went.

"There's an educated Indian—nit," said he.
"He's been to a school for four years, and has
had fine instruction in theology, and here he is
thirsting for the blood of the only pretty girl
that ever lived in this God-forsaken mud corral."

When the cowman entered Carmelita's
room, he found that the change of apparel
had been successfully accomplished. Carmelita
had donned the high-topped boots, the blue
trousers, the red shirt and handkerchief, and
the wide sombrero of Faustino, and he had
put on her clothes, and tied a shawl over
his head. Carmelita had tucked her long black
hair under the sombrero, and at a safe distance and in the darkness, was in little danger
of detection.

"How am I to get away from here after you

are gone? And will it be safe for me to go and leave Alicia?" asked Faustino.

"I'll try to fetch your togs back with me after I get the girl safe to my camp; and when I come back, Alicia must come with us, for these howling hoodoos will be so hot when they find they can't kill Carmelita, that they will kill any of the rest of us they can get their hands on. But we must be tripping, my pretty maid," said he to Carmelita.

Neither of the Indian girls understood more than half of what Wentworth said to them, for while they had both spent a year in an Indian school, their command of the English, or the Spanish language was imperfect. But Carmelita understood the gestures that accompanied the words, and after pressing a long kiss upon the lips of her strangely-clad sweetheart, she pulled the sombrero over her eyes, and followed Wentworth down the ladder.

Wentworth's conversation with the English-speaking Indian, and the big, round dollar that accompanied it, had paved the way for an easy exit, and he and the girl walked out of the pueblo unchallenged. They reached the chuck-wagon in safety, and Carmelita was soon safely

within the covered wagon, while Wentworth
explained the situation to his partner, and the
two began devising ways to rescue Alicia and
Faustino.

It was finally arranged that the men should
return to the pueblo, taking Faustino's clothes
with them. Carmelita was compelled to take
off the clothes and don a suit that belonged to
Wentworth's partner. Then the two cowboys
went back to the pueblo, Wentworth indulging
in the picturesque language he used, which was
a mixture of the English he studied in school,
and the peculiar *patois* of the cow country.

When they entered the pueblo, and had gotten a few steps within the plaza, they were
halted by the Indian Wentworth had talked
with.

Wentworth's partner could speak Spanish,
and he answered the Indian, when he asked
why they were there.

"When my friend left the pueblo with the
Mexican boy, they were in great haste to leave
the *bruja*, and my friend forgot his horse, and
the Mexican, Faustino, forgot both his horse,
which he left in the corrals, and his revolver,
which he left in the house of Carmelita. We

will get those things, and leave this bundle,
which contains some presents for Alicia, and go
again at once. Faustino has now gone into
the house for his revolver, and he will soon be
ready to go."

"How could the Mexican, Faustino, get
into the house of Carmelita?" asked the Indian,
suspiciously. "The house is guarded, and I
have not seen him pass."

"He entered from the outside ladder, from
the side that does not face the plaza," answered
the cowman.

"But that side is guarded, too," said the
Indian.

"No doubt; but the guard would let him
enter when he knew what he desired. But we
will go to the house and ask him to make haste,
as it is time for us to be away," and slipping
two more dollars into the guard's hand, the
two cowboys climbed the ladder to the room
where Alicia and the Mexican were. Several
bushy heads popped out of dark door-ways, and
several pairs of eyes gazed at them, but they
were not hindered, and the Indian guard, in his
own language, explained why they had come.
An Indian went to the corral and brought out

the two horses, holding them ready for Faustino and Wentworth, as they were anxious to see them out of the pueblo for good."

The two white men entered the room and found its occupants sitting in silence. Tears were in the eyes of the girl, and Faustino wore a very sad expression. It was no time for conjectures or explanations, however, and Wentworth threw the bundle to the Mexican, and said:

"Shinny into them togs as quick as you can, and let's get out of this. Hurry! Those red devils are getting mighty suspicious, and they won't stand monkeying with."

Faustino took the bundle, retired to the dark room that opened off the living room, and soon returned, clothed in his own apparel. Then all four of them climbed down the ladder, Alicia carrying the bundle that now contained her sister's garments.

"Why does Alicia go with you?" asked the Indian guard, who stood at the foot of the ladder.

"We thought it well for her to visit at our camp, as she has done many times before," answered the cowman who could speak Spanish.

"What has she wrapped up, that she carries upon her back?" again asked the suspicious Indian.

"She has food which we have bought from her. We are on a journey with our cattle, and our food is almost gone."

"It looks much like the bundle which you had before, and which you said was a present for Alicia," argued the suspicious guide.

"A toad-stool looks much like a mush-room, but it is quite different," said Wentworth. "Look here: we have treated you well and given you money, and you know there is danger in this place to-night. If you are our friend, you will not keep us longer."

The Indian sulkily stood to one side, and the little party passed on. They hastened over the sandy soil to the camp, and when once there, Faustino and Carmelita effected a change of garments, the boy standing behind the wagon and passing her garments in to her and she passing his out under the wagon flap, while the others discussed ways and means at a little distance. They decided that it would not be safe for the Mexican and Carmelita to remain at the wagon, and as they expected that the flight of the supposed *bruja* would soon be discovered, Wentworth saddled his ponies ready for any emergency.

Faustino believed that it would be safer for him and Carmelita to go at once to his mother's house, but Wentworth argued that as soon as Carmelita's disappearance became known, mounted Indians would search the road that led there. Faustino then suggested that they should go to the home of a friend of his, who was a wood-cutter living in an isolated place beyond the cliff dwellings of the Pu-Ye; and this was decided upon. Carmelita kissed her sister, hands were shaken all around, and the Mexican and his sweetheart mounted ponies, and started up the lonely road through the valley of Santa Clara. They rode in silence for a few miles, when, without warning, a bullet whizzed by the head of the girl, and then another shot was heard, singing close to their ears.

The flight of the girl had been discovered; it was suspected that in some way Faustino had helped her to escape, and a party of mounted Indians had set out up the river to overtake them. Just as this party had gotten on to the little mesa south of the

Mexican village of Guchepangue, one of them
had heard the beat of the horses' hoofs down
in the valley on the road to the cañon, and
they had ridden until they were close enough to
discern that one of the riders was a girl, and an
Indian girl at that.

The ponies ridden by Faustino and Carmelita sprang away in a mad gallop, as soon as
the shots were fired, and the Indians spurred
after them in hot pursuit. The sky was partly
clouded and the moon only came out occasionally. When it shone, it enabled the pursued to
ascertain the actions of their pursuers, and it
showed them also that their pursuers were not
gaining on them very rapidly. But with every
burst of moonlight came a shower of bullets,
and with their heads bent down to their horses'
necks, the fugitives raced on and prayed for
darkness. The hoofs of the horses struck fire
from the stones, branches of the small trees
almost scraped the riders from their saddles,
and there was imminent danger that the horses
would stumble and fall into some of the *arroyos*
and ditches on the way. The pursuing Indians,
now being out of the region of any Mexican
settlement, began to yell, and to shout curses

at the *bruja;* and so the mad little band raced up the cañon. Little Indian huts were passed, gullies were leaped, the horses tore madly through thickets, and still the frightened girl and her lover clung to their ponies, and raced on, in hope of finding safety in some way that the good spirits might send to them.

The road to the cliff dwellings is long and hard and steep, but it can be shortened in miles if one will ride up the bed of a mountain torrent, that is dry in all but the rainy season. Up this water-way Faustino and the girl turned their horses, and up it, also, rode their pursuers, shouting like demons, and firing their revolvers ahead of them at random. The horses of the Indians were not as swift as the others, however, and the boy and girl gained rapidly, as their horses, now wildly frightened, tore up the bed of the torrent. When the top was reached, the moon shone out for an instant, and Faustino turned in his saddle and fired down the gulch. A yell answered his bullet, and he rode on, cheered with the hope that he might have hit one of the band of pursuers.

Some of the Indians failed to reach the mesa that was at the upper end of the torrent bed,

"Faustino tired down the gulch."

because their horses could not stand the strain, and the number of pursuers was reduced to a half-dozen. Two of them soon fell out of the race, but the other four clattered away over the stony mesa, hoping to get a shot at the Indian girl before she should disappear.

"Can we reach the house of your friend, Faustino?" gasped the girl.

"Let us hope so, sweetheart. Let us not be without hope, and do you always look ahead and never look back, and thus it will be better with us," said the boy. And turning in his saddle, he fired another shot at one of his pursuers, who had forged ahead of the others and was rapidly gaining upon the fugitives. The bullet struck the Indian's horse in the forehead and killed it, and left its rider powerless to continue the pursuit. The other Indians were a considerable distance farther away, and the hoof-beats of their horses sounded fainter and fainter, showing that the horses were becoming exhausted, and the riders losing ground. The horses ridden by the Mexican and the girl were bathed in lather, frothing at the mouth, and trembling like aspens from fatigue and fright.

Presently the riders came in sight of the big, white cliffs that frown down so solemnly upon the little valley, and they knew they had reached the old cliff-dwellings of the Pu-Ye. Faustino turned his pony directly toward the cliff, and urged his companion to hasten the speed of her horse.

"Let us not go to the Pu-Ye," said Carmelita. "It is a dark and silent place, and it is said that the spirits of the ancient ones meet there at night, and tell to each other old tales of the time when they dwelt upon the earth as men and women. Let us strive to reach the house of your friend."

"Our horses will soon drop with fatigue, and it is yet four miles to the house of the wood-cutter. If we can reach the cliffs and get into one of the cliff houses, we will have an advantage, for we will be in the shadow, and the men cannot reach us without climbing, and as they climb I can shoot, and you can hurl down rocks."

A couple of hundred yards before they reached the base of the cliff, Carmelita's horse fell, utterly exhausted. Faustino sprang from his saddle, grasped the girl about the waist,

" Up this perilous ascent the boy and girl made their way."

swung her on to his horse, and was mounted
and away again, within a minute. Just before
he reached the cliff his own horse fell, and he
and the girl, hand in hand, began to climb
the ascent.

In the face of the cliff were cut, in some old
age, some slit-like footholds that the prehistoric
inhabitants of the place had used as ladders,
and up this perilous ascent the boy and girl
made their way. They were almost exhausted,
and in a frenzy of excitement, and it was a
marvel that they did not slip and fall. As
they were half-way up the side of the cliff they
heard the yells of the pursuers, who had just
discovered the fallen horse of Carmelita.

"Hasten, sweetheart, and be brave; we are
almost to our place of safety," urged Faustino.
And again they climbed from one niche to another, up the almost perpendicular wall of the
cliff.

They passed the first tier of cliff houses,
but were compelled to stop at the second, as
they were too nearly exhausted to go farther.
Faustino drew himself up to the little entrance-
aperture, and then lifted and pulled the girl
after him; and they sank back into the dust on

the floor in utter exhaustion. The dust of the cliff houses is as fine as flour, and their movements in it caused clouds of it to rise in the little chamber, and settle in their mouths and nostrils and almost stifle them. They lay for a few minutes in utter exhaustion, and then the girl said:

"How long will it be until the men can come to this place."

"They can soon come to the base of the cliff, but it will take them long to climb up here, if they can at all. No shots were fired at us when we were climbing, so they must have been so far behind us that they feared they could not hit us."

The girl put her arm about the neck of the boy, brought his head down upon her bosom, and said:

"Sweetheart of mine, it is but a little time, but the counting of a few numbers, until the men will come upon us and kill us, as they would kill beasts in a trap. If I had done what it was right to do, I would have stayed in the pueblo, and let you go, safe and free upon your way. I have done a great wrong to you to let you lose your life in protecting me, and it is that alone that I grieve for. But before the men come upon us, I want to tell to you again the tale of how much I love you. You are to me the greatest joy in the world, and my love for you has brought me more happiness than was ever known by any woman who ever dwelt upon the earth before. When you were away from me, I have been happy in dreaming of the time when I should be your wife and we should dwell together all the days and nights; and when you have been with me, my happiness was greater than is that of the blessed ones who dwell in the land of Po-so-yemmo in the sun. Sweetheart, you have been all the world to me—all the world, and all the hope and joy and goodness and happiness of the world! I love you, sweetheart, more than I have words to tell. And all the sorrow that I now know is the sorrow of having brought you to the place of your death, when you might have been safe and free, if it had not been for me."

The boy tenderly kissed the girl, pressed her closer to him, and said nothing.

"Do you love me, sweetheart?" asked the girl.

"Better than all the world besides," answered the boy.

"Better than the long years of your life that now will not be lived?" asked the girl.

"Yes, sweet one."

"Better than all hope of the happiness you would have known if your life had been long? Better than the joy of having wife and children, and living to a ripe old age, honored among the people of your kind?"

"Better than all that; better than anything in the world but the joy of loving you."

"Then let the hunters come, for I am ready. We shall be killed together, and together, as spirits, we shall go into that life that lies beyond this. If my creed is true, then will we go together, hand in hand, to the abode of Yo-See in the fair land of the sun. And if the creed of the people of your race is the true one, then together shall we go to that place where all things are justly judged."

A bullet whizzed into the opening of the cave, and shattered the plastering from the ancient stone wall. Faustino arose cautiously, peered out, and saw his pursuers stealthily nearing the face of the cliff. He did not feel like risking a shot at them, preferring to wait until they began to climb the cliff; but he felt about him to learn if any rocks could be found. His hand came in contact with an old *metate* stone, that had served as a hand-mill for the cliff-dwellers, centuries ago, and with further search he found another. He made no noise and he and Carmelita lay prone in the dust, waiting for the Indians to begin to climb.

The Indians skulked for a time about the base of the cliff, holding a parley in a low tone, and then one of them stealthily crawled away, and one of the others began to climb up the rude ladder that led to the cliff houses. When he was about half-way to the entrance, Faustino hurled one of the stones upon him. It struck the Indian, and he fell like a log to the ground. Faustino then took aim at the remaining Indian, fired, and the bullet found its mark, for the Indian yelled, and sank to the ground. The captives were safe for a time, but were much concerned as to what they might expect from the Indian who had stolen away. They believed he would climb to the mesa above them and then climb down, hoping to take them unawares.

"When he comes we must fight him with our hands, for my last bullet is gone," said Faustino.

They lay for a time anxiously peering out of the little porthole-like entrance to see the Indian when he came. Soon they saw one of his feet lowered, very silently and cautiously, feeling for the last foot-niche that he would use before he sprung within the cave. As though guided by the same inspiration, both Faustino and Carmelita made a lunge to grasp the man's leg, and both caught it at once. Excitement lent them strength, and they pulled so vigorously that the man lost his balance and toppled over, but was held from falling by the grasp of his captors. They pulled him into the cave, and in an instant the strong hands of the Mexican boy were choking the life from his struggling body. Faustino crowded the Indian back in the dust, climbed upon him, knelt on his chest, and all the time choked him so hard that the man was almost dead.

"Do not kill him," said Carmelita. "It seems that we may be spared, and if it is to be so, let us not kill. But let us bind him, and then go and leave him."

The Indian had climbed with a knife between his teeth, which had fallen when he was so unexpectedly thrust upon the floor and choked. Carmelita grasped his knife, with it cut a strip from her skirt, and as soon as Faustino could roll the man over, she bound his hands together behind his back with strips of cloth, that held as firmly as though they had been bands of iron. Then they bound his legs together, and gagged him, and he lay silent and motionless, and as harmless as though he had been dead.

" Is not this a joyful time ? " asked Faustino, complacently gazing upon his fallen antagonist and grinning like a schoolboy with a new kite.

" Be silent," said Carmelita. " The ones below may not be hurt so much as we think and may come at any time. Ah, I hear one say that all their cartridges are gone."

" Then we are safe," almost shouted Faustino. " If they cannot shoot we can climb down and I can fight them with this knife and with stones. Oh, is not this a joyful time? And will not my *compadre*, Pablo Barillo, open wide his mouth when I tell him all the things that have befallen us this night?" And Faustino rose to his feet and administered a vigorous kick to the body of the prostrate Indian who lay bound before him.

"But we are not yet safe and free, and away from the men who would kill us," answered Carmelita. "At any time other men may come here, and they may have guns and many cartridges, and fresh horses, and we have nothing but this *metate* stone and a knife."

"It is true," said Faustino, sobering. "We are yet in danger, and if we are to escape from here, it must be soon. And I am in so great thirst that I can scarcely open my lips."

"Is it safe for us to climb down, and pass the men below, and go away?" asked Carmelita.

"Is it not much better for us to climb up to the top of the mesa, and then go away into the next valley?"

"I could climb no more," said Carmelita, wearily. "If I can but get down, and escape those below, and have strength to get away before more men come, it will be all that I can do."

"But if we climb down, the men below may grasp you and do you harm while we are striving to pass them," said Faustino.

Carmelita considered soberly for a moment, and then said:

"The men of my people believe me to be a *bruja*, and while they will lose their lives to kill *brujas*, they fear them more than they fear all other things in the world. It is best to make them fear me, and escape through their fear."

"But how?" asked her companion.

Instead of replying, Carmelita put her head out of the opening and called out: "Ho, you below! It is I, Carmelita the *bruja*, who speaks! Where is Lo-Ha, the coward who climbed to the top of the mesa and then climbed down the stone ladder to kill us? Answer me or I will cause you to die in an instant, for I am a *bruja* and can kill."

The thought that the powerful *bruja* might kill them had not entered their thick heads before, but as soon as it did, they were tremendously frightened, and they answered at once:

"We know not where Lo-Ha is. A little time ago we saw him climb down the cliff, and at once he became silent and we know not how it is with him."

"You know not, you fools? Then will I tell you. I touched Lo-Ha with my hands, and at once he turned to dust, and now he is lying as dust, upon the floor of this cave. Now tell me how it is with you, and if you do not tell, your breath shall at once leave your bodies forever."

"We are much hurt," answered one of the Indians. "One of us had a hand shot off, and the other his shoulder broken by the rock."

"And now if you do not at once get beyond my sight, I will change you both into beasts. You, who have only a broken shoulder, can walk, and you other have one strong arm left. You can both walk, so get down the steep place, and out of my sight and hearing at once, else is this the last night you shall ever live upon the earth."

This command was what Michael J. Wentworth would have called a "sky-high bluff," and the two lovers waited in great suspense to ascertain what effect it would have. But it "worked." And the Indians at once went to a considerable distance. Then the lovers climbed down the perilous ladder, and hand in hand, took up their weary journey to home and safety.

All the long hours of the dreary night they toiled on, sometimes dropping from fatigue and exhaustion, but each time rising and going forward again, for hope was with them and it gave them strength. And, as the sun was coming up over the peaks of the Santa Fé range, a jaded Mexican boy with bleeding hands and feet, led a fainting Indian girl wearing tattered moccasins and a skirt cut into strips, into a little adobe house that looked from a low mesa down upon the shifting channel of the Rio Grande del Norte.

There was a startled old Mexican mother, and a wide-mouthed boy of a brother, and a jerky story told between smiles and tears; then a hot breakfast and a long, long, delicious sleep. Then baths in rain-water and amole soap, and another hot meal. When all was said and done, the old mother took the Indian girl to her heart and wept over her and the boy, alternately; and she gave her consent to their union, and began planning a future for them that consisted, first of a trip to the church at Santa Cruz, and the building of a new adobe cottage next, and a *fandango grande* to end it all up with, in a meet and becoming manner. And Faustino the herder and Carmelita the half-breed, rested, refreshed, fed, and clothed in clean garments, were made man and wife; and they now dwell in a little adobe *casita* that is made cheery all day long by the songs of the wife and the cooing of a little brown babe, that sits upon the cemented floor and plays with bright red *chili* peppers for toys.

www.ingramcontent.com/pod-product-compliance
Lightning Source LLC
Chambersburg PA
CBHW020902020726
47497CB00005B/1517